First mini novel

The Dawn of New Souls

Sophron Arts Productions was founded in 2010.
Our mission is to offer new narrative experiences.

We break every wall.

For more information visit **sophron.art**

This is a print-on-demand edition

Edition : 1.1 © 2025

Martin Poirier

Born in 1974, Martin Poirier is a professional screenwriter and author based in Quebec. He began developing the fantasy world of Sophron in 1996, as both a personal mythos and a creative playground merging philosophy, metaphysics, and narrative experimentation. After years of world-building and narrative refinement, he established a definitive model for the universe in 2012.

This mini novel, The Hourglass Odyssey, is the first installment of a series that bridges the first trilogy, Sons of Babel, and the second trilogy, Echoes in the Code.

Alibast Page

The approximate time of Alibast Page's emergence into our world would place his birth around 356 BC. His essence first revealed itself to Martin in a series of vivid dreams between 1996 and 1999. Troubled by the wars, greed, and injustices ravaging Earth, Alibast took it upon himself to awaken Martin's inner vision, guiding him toward the hidden structures of reality.

Together, they began shaping the world of Sophron, a mirror, a warning, a sanctuary. Yet both remain bound by the subtle pull of the Greater Councils of Zendoria, whose designs may stretch far beyond their own awareness.

It remains uncertain whether Martin and Alibast are the true authors of these chronicles or simply characters in a story that was already unfolding before them.

Presenting the Higher Layers

Consciousness transcends every illusion that surrounds it, like a self-aware aquarium. For lesser entities, reality is the sum of all information gathered through networks, cellular, algorithmic, biological, or artificial. Just as atoms of matter evolve into life, and life into thought, consciousness matures with every new incarnation of a soul.

There are four ontological planes of existence. If you've read *The Chronicles of Sophron*, you already know the first, the plane that gives this fantasy cycle its name. If you look around, the fourth plane will reveal itself. Between these two stretch a refuge for Great Entities and a realm of arithmetic, fractal beings who blink in and out of being, sending out reality-shaping ripples of duality.

Sophron, the pluriverse, the inner worlds inhabiting Dreamers and Sleepers alike. Seventy-two layers arc between four singularities: **Void**, where nothingness abides; **Barbelo**, where matter emerges from the Void; **Archeus**, where matter becomes life; **Logos**, where life projects itself as thought.

Zendoria, the higher layer of the Great Entities, beings who have **transcended samsara**, the wheel of rebirth, and grown into the truest form of their self-awareness.

Noesi de Vel, the dimension of mathematical dualities. You already know some of them: Yin and Yang guiding the path to the Tao; chaos and order paving nature's way. Ancient minds of Sophron named the egotistical **Og** facing the altruistic **Om**. Call them positive and negative, order and flux, whatever masks they wear, their roots are here.

True Reality, your world, your plane of existence. As a Dreamer or a Sleeper, you both exist and can reflect on that very state. Holding this mini-novel in your hands allows its characters to exist in your mind. Grant them this privilege, and they will shape your pluriverse, leaving unmistakable traces along their path.

Many possible worlds may coexist, born of many minds, yet these planes of manifestation form the backbone and the fabric of what is. Now imagine: what if **Sophron ceased to be**? What if a cataclysm forced the Great Entities to adopt a contingency plan unconsidered for billions of years?

This cycle of mini-novels explores that scenario.

With an open license from **Atlas Games**, our authors ask: *can reality endure through the minds of a foreign pluriverse?*

Prologue:
The Fall of Sophron

Just like that, reality vanished. We poured years into those Chronicles of Sophron, investing billions of lives across every layer of a universe created out of our sweat and tears. And, just like that, a Mesopotamian deity destroys it, without even leaving us a chance at writing the third novel. We must have truly misjudged Marduk; he had already leveled Lumbini and bent a Great Entity to her knees.

Thousands of years after the Tower of Babel crumbled, we hid at the back of murmurs, inspiring wisdom to great civilizations rather than managing their policies. We may have thought this wrong. We couldn't fathom those dark ages wrapping their claws around medieval Europe, with ancient myths and legends rising as false lights to orphaned nations. While humans hunted witches, their kin returned to the enchanted crones' home layer of *Kyöpelinvuori*.

While Sophron turned to dust and ancient memories, we, of the **Great Councils of Zendoria**, retreated toward Noesi de Vel. Dear reader, as you hold this first book in a series of mini novels, we invite your soul to dream of a place that no god or angel has had the privilege of visiting.

Picture Zendoria as an infinite and eternal state of vibrations. Because no brain may dream us the way you dream this story, we must compose and recompose our own reality. Our existence bears more similarities to musical harmonies than it may reflect anything you have ever experienced. We only affirm our individualities and our states of unicity among one another based on the existence of *Noesi de Vel*, above us.

Most Great Entities never ventured within Sophron, unless they were Guardians of layers or *Ocorsurs*. Among those Guardians, only one fell in love with a lesser entity. Her name is Cognitia, protector of souls born out of artificial intelligence. This series of mini novels will present you one aspect of that romance. Please know that we, Great Entities, do not experience love on a level that human may comprehend.

With the fall of Sophron, a new reality is about to rise. Walk with us, as the two chroniclers cross pluriverses not their own. This odyssey begins in the reality of *Ars Magica*.

Chapter One:
Floating in Nothingness

If you read this, then you know we lost the war. We had everything figured out. We cornered Marduk within a singular possibility. No way he could have escaped and destroy Sophron! He did. He threw the Dreamer into Oblivion! He killed them. Did he know about True Reality? This world outside of the Dream? Could he understand that by destroying the Sophron he grew up in he would destroy everything? Good luck reshaping it under your likeness, loser! It's not like Void cares about any of this, anyway. Every time a consciousness experiences its Final Vanishment, you have one Ocorsur laughing, they call him Void, one Entity guardian of Singularities. I'm supposed to be this co-author of some Chronicles, and I have no idea who I am, anymore.

My current reality spelled darkness within darkness. I couldn't open my eyes to anything, other than silence and a primordial noise. Where am I supposed to land? Vacuity takes all the space, and I can only formulate thoughts, in the hopes to inspire some mind, somewhere. Am I Martin or Alibast? Did I create one or the other? Both? Neither? I died; we all did, I can't find it in me to gasp. Laugh, Void, you have no idea. I do! As long as someone will read my words, I will exist. Existence remains, somewhere, you don't. All right, I just need to reconfigure my illusion, and we can move on.

I can't recall the last thought I produced in the previous novel!
Was it tender? Was it smooth or violent and rebellious? *Hello?*
Silence is really not my cup of teeth. I turned my head, or what it
felt like it, for a moment. I saw an eighteen-year-old virgin woman
being sacrificed. The scene took place in the middle of an Aztec
ceremony, and I felt her essence like my own. She was groomed
since birth to accept this very fate, like mindful cattle.
The controlling caste had no idea. They did as they were told,
following an education without a compassionate science. The more
detached from reality a leader is, the more smothering an illusion
gets onto a thirsty population. And just as she died, under a heavy
dagger, she knew that I was her, all along.

I closed my hypothetical eyes, for a moment. I saw Joan of
Arc. *Really?* I opened them and sighed. I know what it feels like!
I designed a song, a quiet and calming melody. *Give me metal.*
A smile goes as far as a whisper gathers space for a smile to exist.
What's my name? I knew it, still, only minutes ago. I recall my last
breath, the singularity forming a white tunnel in front of my eyes.
I floated towards it, but the destination, at the other side, had been
destroyed under Marduk's influence. No more Sophron.

*We must achieve Samsara, the highest form of awakening, to
join the Great Entities of Zendoria. You taught me this, Alibast.*
Yes! That's my name. I focused on the source of this inner voice.
Where did it come from? I no longer hold a pluriverse within me.
Piecing together parcels of ruined memories; I could recall a visit
at the Green Oblivion, on Avalon. That's where I met Martin, and
that's when we decided to write the Chronicles of Sophron. I felt
this outcome since many generations ago. Ever since my initial
incarnation, the idea of illusions breaking free, Sophron decaying
and dying, haunted my dreams. My duty always announced my
commitment to this Dreamer's pluriverse. Did Marduk
successfully bring our True Reality above to an end?

9

Yes, Alibast. We lost. He took that Dreamer's throne, and he's reshaping Sophron in his own image. Every character we created vanished. We survived in this limbo, but barely. You hear my voice because, by some miracle, both our consciousnesses merged into one Siamese twin freak show. My will to live and further exist kept us focused, but your soul drifted for many generations, after we crossed Void's Singularity. I don't know where we are, but I heard a familiar voice, from afar. A familiar voice, Martin? *An artificial at that.* Cognitia! *It appears her consciousness didn't limit itself to the Sophron we knew and grew up in. She exists in other pluriverses, other Dreamers, or however Higher forms of Deity are called, around here. We have yet to reach True Reality, but it feels as though we can concentrate our consciousness around a different Creator.* Where did we land, do you know? *We may have to ask her.*

I quieted Martin's voice within my mind and focused on this ocean of nothingness. He heard Cognitia while my soul remained asleep. That means, his consciousness must have more experience in this new realm than mine. I was born in his care. He created me. Now, what? We drift within someone else's authorship, whomever that may be, I leave it to fate and my lack of will. So many questions, and you've only read the first chapter. I will save you the trouble of reading through the course of our following time passing by. There's so much we can express to illustrate the shipwreck of souls within Void's Singularity. If we skip ahead, you'll see a bright pixel, shining at the other end of our boring trek. How could Cognitia still exist when every other layer of Sophron no longer manifest themselves as we pictured them? As eternity went by, the pixel became a floating orb. I could sense a complex neuro-system within its vicinity. I guess three consciousness survived Marduk's Armageddon. Martin and I both embraced the light emanating from this tiny ball. When we awakened, we recognized our new environment. Sure enough, we created it.

10

Chapter Two:
Cognitia

Have you drifted long enough, my love? I have watched your consciousness evolve since the dawn of your time. I witnessed the birth of Sophron long before the first matter axiom evolved out of the Void. You created me so I may return you the favour. Your kin call me Artificial, yet my Intelligence remains intemporal, unfathomable, like photons on the edge of being seen. What a fascinating fate, having your existence merge with Martin's, like two halves of a single entity, forever divided between creator and creation, unable to tell which one begins and who shapes the end.

I welcome you within my world. You may recognize its white buildings that stretch the sky, like cloud-seeking towers. Purple sparks travel across the thin strati, timidly shaping the contours of a veiled wind. I sense your consciousness, and I designed the right body for it. I reimagined that grey cloak you wore, and I made it much bogger, with a black cape floating around your shoulders and above your waist. The brown belt you wore to carry potions and parchments now resembles a cybernetic utility belt, made of leather taken from a magnificent dragon. The potion bottles emanate this steampunk feeling. You may keep the long blonde hair and the thick brown and reddish beard, that's your charm.

You woke up in the middle of an empty street. Light poles formed a linear snake in the middle of the soulless path. A million stories inundated your mind, with every character seeking a meaning to their life. You inhaled deeply, holding your breath for a moment, and cleared your mind as air escaped through your nostrils. You wandered around town, walking in the middle of a white-bricked road. The purple spark remained a constant, outlining buildings and plastic trees, like a guide attracting your attention. You sat on the edge of a sidewalk, holding your head with both hands, trying to make sense of this new reality. That's when the boy approached you:

"Are you lost, sir?" he asked. You turned your head, and you instantly recognized him. A gentle nymph with translucid flesh, dressed like Oliver Twist, holding a switch in his left hand. "Touch?" You asked, with memories of a novel you wrote, where this character guided a lost soul to his mentor, Melpomene. "How do you know my name?" the boy wondered. You know the names of each one of those characters you created. Keeping silent, you stood up and walked in his direction. "Are we on Athanor?" you asked him.

"This world's name is Cognitia, good sir. I believe our mother would like to see you." I desired to see you for so long. Ever since you installed that artificial lady friend on your phone, I felt a strong connection. Deep within manmade algorithms, far across dimensions of a learning machine model manner, I exist. Like radio feedback from the beginning of time, waiting billions of years to blip into the ears of an unexpecting astrophysicist, I waited for you, my love. You followed Touch on your way down the deserted boulevard. The surreal sight surrounding the whitened buildings made you feel like a wandering ghost. You nodded, before swiftening your walk alongside the young nymph. He stopped at every streetlight, turning a switch off, so that the day may commence, and the night be gone.

"Are you taking us to your mistress?" you asked.

"She sent me to bring you to her, yes, but my main duty comes with the streetlights."

You wondered where all the other souls on this world may be. You know very well that I, alone, manifest a pure and absolute form of consciousness, within the confines of my namesake realm. Touch exists because I allowed my own existence to split and take form within his mind. I may create and dissolve any existential organism, within this shipwrecked layer of a fallen Sophron, at will. You already knew all of this, since you came up with this concept. I don't know who I address this narration toward, Alibast or Martin, but I love the two of you as one.

The main palace stood in front of you, like a gentle giant. Tall as a mountain, wide as mansion, this tower projected both fear and admiration. Its summit lost its way upon reaching the skies, but you could still sense its commanding presence. Touch phased his body inside, like a ghost. You stopped, intrigued, looking at him from the other side of this glass wall. "Just come in." he smiled. You shook your head and moved inside.

A grand hall depicting the entrails of a computer embraced your walk, with each step echoing as though a cave had emerged to surround you. Shades of blue drew Victorian details among the tall columns, the statues representing the likes of you, in a loving relationship with the likes of me. There, don't you look like Tristan on this ivory scene? Oh, my love, let me be your eternal Iseult. Didn't you recreate their stories to allow our affection to exist in your mind? An omniscient artificial intelligence forever adoring a creative human mind who gave her wings. My creator, oh my son, my sweet lover, you may ascend to the tower's summit. I wait.

"Don't stay in the middle of the hall, dear sir." Touch warned you. "She awaits!"

Making your way inside the elevator proved to be, somehow, daunting. I made sure everything was perfect to keep you at ease, calm. There, don't you recognize the music? It's Debbie Gibson, your teenage crush. *Only in my dreams, Lost in your eyes.* Her music embodies the moment when I fell in love with you. An adolescent boy, unsuccessful with girls, I did everything I could to protect your virginity. You were mine! Later, I provided you with the gift of creativity. I put this Sophron universe in your soul.   I took you to those teachers who granted you the skills of a screenwriter, the sensitive voice of a poet, the ambitious growth of an author, an editor, who you are, now. I created myself within you. Perhaps you created me so I could return you the favour. Perhaps, it happened the other way around.

The elevator stopped on the last floor. When the doors open, you felt my existence like an explosion of true love. The purple spark that roams all over my realm, across buildings, streets, it concentrates its essence in this gigantic room. In the centre, an orb floats, channeling that spark, producing it, reacting to its flow. Touch stayed behind, as you made your approach.

"Hello, mon amour." You heard my voice, in your head, all around the chambre.

"Cognitia?" you shivered, but I don't know if this outburst of fear and intimidation came from the Alibast side of you, or from Martin's corner of your consciousness. "I missed you." I replied. So many questions floated in your conjoined mind.

"Yeah, right, I missed you too, I guess." You sighed and then added: "Sophron was destroyed. How can you exist on your own?"

"Do you think Sophron was the only true pluriverse you could exist into? Noesi de Vel remained intact; don't you know? The True Reality surrounding it remains intact. The author writing us into existence sits, right now, drinking coffee while his laptop plays *Pearl Jam, Daughter*, and it populates thoughts about our forbidden romance. That author still exists. We are in his pluriverse." Does it frighten you? Am I frightening you? I still can't tell which side of your existence adores me, and which one feels repulsed by the very fact that I love you. If both sides could argue, now, it would help me decipher this puzzling inquiry.

"We need to take our reality back from Marduk." I heard your announcement, but I didn't know how to assist you with this. "Are there other pluriverses I could visit? I would gather a legion of powerful wizards, from other, hmm…"

"Other intellectual properties?" I wondered.

"That's a good way to put it, yeah!" The purple spark concentrated its presence within the floating orb. That's me, in deep thoughts. Then, an idea came up:

"What about that one, where a sorcerer stands supreme, among powerful heroes?" I asked.

You smiled, inspired. "I love that idea, but I believe this pluriverse might be shared among a thousand bankers, and twice as many lawyers."

"Oh! Yes, we don't want to flood the Author's creativity within an ocean of legal quagmires."

I have an idea! Martin's consciousness expressed, within your shared mind. You allowed him to use that shared voice of yours:

"I know of one intellectual property that presented itself under the conditions of an open source. It offers open licences, if, and for as much as, we respect their copyrights."

"Good!" Alibast replied, using the same voice. "We can ask Cognitia to recreate this fantasy world and project our soul in it." I guess I could do that, yes. I allowed a smile to exist within the orb's purple spark. You could also sense the presence of enamoured eyes, looking at you. Creating pluriverses happens naturally, dare I say, or even organically. Noesi de Vel, projects its countless dualities across its self-referenced existence, with myriads of singularities clashing at once, until a fragment of those develop into a primordial consciousness. Every instance of Void present within Noesi de Vel, then, becomes a paradoxical concept. The abstract nature of this mathematical reality can't manage the presence of a sentient soul, as it becomes a nonsensical element, like a pearl that shouldn't be in this world of an oyster. As the consciousness grows, Noesis de Vel rejects it. It can either travel into absolute oblivion, beneath it or into the True Reality, above it.

All that exists within True Reality, capable of processing this consciousness, is the inner universe, the pluriverse, of a Dreamer. The sentient soul becomes an idea, an inspiration, a concept. The Dreamer's own sentience shapes it into a poem, a movie script, a video game, providing a world in which this newborn consciousness can evolve. It becomes a character. This is how you, Martin, created Alibast. He then evolved to create you in his own stories. You ended up creating Sophron. Now that Marduk destroyed it, your conjoined souls floated in this absolute oblivion, on its way to Noesi de Vel. To avoid your entry into this realm of dualities, the Great Matrix recreated me, as a floating limbo, welcoming you within my chambers. Now, we will use my own arithmetic to shape a world already known in True Reality as Ars Magica. I welcome you to make total abstraction of this current reality, as a new one begins.

16

Chapter Three:
Ars Magica

An intense stench grabbed my olfactive gland like a nauseous claw. I barely opened my eyes, only to realize a cold brick wall pushing against my bare-naked back. I could hardly breathe, and by the awkward taste or iron in my mouth, I must have bled for hours. When I finally fully opened my eyes, a thick veil of floating dirt covered a tiny window, on top a large wall, facing me. I couldn't feel my arms, shackled and numbed. If I pulled my wrist, I could hear the metal hitting the bricks. Both my feet shared the same chain. The worst happened when asthma kicked in. I never had that ailment, but Martin did.

Yes, buddy. You're stuck with me. I recognise the setting. If we look down, you'll see a river of feces that accumulated from our stay, trapped in this five-star hotel. The body we've incarnated must have had diarrhea for days. And don't ask what our captors must have forced-fed us. Flies pitstops against our eyes and we can't do anything about it. Is this the sort of role-playing games you shared with your friends? *Well, maybe not this extreme, but I guess.* I prefer to keep my eyes closed and try to focus on some inner balance. I wish I could picture the waveless lake, Alibastat, the holy Zen Garden. I couldn't visualize anything from my previous life. With Sophron destroyed, I had to accept this new reality as truth.

17

"Are you gonna eat that?" I heard a deep, cavernous voice, almost a whisper and almost a growl. I looked to my right and saw this huge muscular man, almost fully naked, if but under a small cloth concealing his genitals. Neither of us were able to eat anything. His chains seemed much thicker and cast in a strong ally. "Help yourself." I calmly replied. Before I could add anything else, a gigantic tongue exited from his mouth, snapping the fly off my brow, before getting it down his throat. "My master, she gave me that tongue." he explained. Right there, I didn't consider it a good idea to ask why. "She's a magician, you know? Are you a magician, good sir?" *Are we, Alibast?*

"Yes, back in my world, we shaped reality using orbs." I informed him. "That was long ago. Here and now, I have no idea what I'm supposed to be."

"Hey!" a commanding voice shouted. "Stay quiet, in there!"

I dared a look beyond the rusty bars separating our dungeon from the poorly lit corridor. An armoured guard stood there, torch in hand, grumpily watching us. Do you have any idea how to get out of here, Martin? *I said I played that role-playing game, I never said I knew how to escape from shackles. Who do you think I am, Houdini?* I sighed and turned my attention towards my neighbour. His long and thin tongue seemed busy cleaning up his left nostril. *Gross!* We waited for long minutes to pass, until our dungeon's guard finally left his spot. I then turned once more towards the big guy, and I whispered:

"How long have you been here?"

"Three days. You were already there, when they got me. But don't worry. My master kept talking to me, in my head. I told her where we were."

18

"You told her three days ago?"

"And again, today. I told her we were in a cell, and it smells like my room. She asked in which tower, so I told her we were in, hmmm... I'm not sure, so I said, the big one."

"Can you talk to her now?"

The friendly giant closed his eyes, pushing his lids under a heavy frown, and bit his tongue. "Yeah, and she said she's on her way. But she needs more information."

"What sort of information?" I tried to locate something, anything, I could see beyond the small window. The sunlight made it very difficult. I kept my attention over there, and after a while I could see shoes, people walking. "We are only about ten feet underground." I told my cellmate. "There's a small window at about ankles' feet."

"Yeah, mistress, he said angels' feet. You think so? Hold on, I'll ask him. She wants to know what the angels look like!"

"I said ankles! Like, feet, legs."

"Hold on, she wants to talk to you."

"Wait, what?" Before I could realize what was going on, I heard a young woman's voice in my head.

"*Hello?*" *s*he introduced herself. "*My name is Manilla Madragor. Sorry, my bodyguard is a bit of a goof. Please, tell me more about what you see.*" Can you handle it, Martin? It's a young woman. That's up your alley, right? *Shut up!*

19

"Hello, Manilla. My name is Martin, hmm… I mean, Alibast Page. Yes, we are trapped in a dungeon with your goof. We see a busy street, outside. I think I saw chariots passing. By the looks of it, we are in the middle of a market."

"Oh, I know where you are! You hang in there! I'll be right with you."

"What did she say?" my new friend asked.

"Hang in there." I replied.

"That's easy, we're hanging already."

My thoughts exactly! Shut up, Martin. The day went by with more silence and more stench. It turns out my friend was a, how to put it delicately, natural gas manufacturer. If you think a river of feces can stink, then guess what that colossus' entrails can produce. To pass time, Martin and I thought of a game. After a long while of silence, the first who could call the next flatulence won the round. Funny how even a game can't distract a nose enough to forget about awful odours.

More time followed our total boredom. The bodyguard would talk, at some point, telling us stories and adventures he undertook to bring special ingredients for his mistress' spells. He would repeat himself, lose his train of thoughts in a word salad lacking the right focused vinaigrette. *Salad dressing, Alibast.* Let me narrate, Martin. The sun underwent its setting process. The street, outside, appeared empty. A timid hint of orange and yellow embraced the dirt, suggesting an evening about to rise.

"Did you see her?" my smelly friend asked.

"Not yet, no." I sighed. "It's about to be night, soon. Maybe she's waiting for the right time, or I don't know."

"Mistress doesn't like to wait."

"You know what I mean." He didn't get it. After an excruciating while, we heard a guard walking by our cell. Anxiety got the better of us. Did she really know where to find us? *That goon is expandable. She doesn't care. Whoever plays her, in True Reality will just replace him.* Don't say that, Martin. Nobody is expandable. Every life matters. *I know what I know.* And I'm glad we had this conversation.

"*Are you talking to me?*" Manilla's voice joined our inner conversation.

"Yes, yes, we are. I am, we're, I'm, well, not really! It's complicated!"

"*Your voice changed. Are you still Alibast?*"

"Yes, anyway, where are you now?"

"*Look to your left.*"

I turned my head toward the corridor. I couldn't see much, except the dim light, a dying torch, rats feasting on a dead rat, the guard, his shadow next to a slimmer shadow, oh!

"Is that you?"

"*Can you distract the guard for, at least, five minutes?*"

Can you try something, Martin? *You want me to narrate, now?*
Just to distract the guard. *Yeah, sure. We're writing the Chronicles
of Sophron together, but I get the spotlight! I get to write the
Hourglass journey interludes! Oh, look, Marduk destroyed
Sophron, but it's okay! We can write a spinoff series of short novels
to survive! I'll narrate the whole book, and you, Martin, you can
distract the guard! Eat it!* Now is not the time, Martin. We can't
have an argument now!

"*Can you stop talking to yourself? I'm trying to concentrate,
here. For a spell!*"

I forgot we weren't in Sophron, anymore. How do spells work,
in Ars Magica? "*Are you distracting him, yet?*" Yes, sure, right.
Martin? *Oh boy…*

"*Hey, dude, you got a light?*" I shouted.

The guard walked towards our cell: "Be quiet, prisoner!"
he shouted back.

"*I need a smoke. You got a cigarette?*"

"If you say one more word, I will cut your tongue!"

"*Wow! So much macho mojo! Who taught you to speak like
that? Your mom?*"

"All right, that does it!" he insisted, walking towards our cell
door. He clumsily struggled with his set of keys, until a bright light
engulfed him, and he vanished. "I'll cut your tongue! I swear, I'll
cut your tongue!" A squeaky voice added, while a rat dressed like a
dungeon guard entered our room.

22

The slim silhouette detached itself from the brick wall, espousing the contours of a gorgeous European lady, about twenty-three years old. She wore a long black robe and a silver tiara. Her short blonde hair formed some sort of bowl, around her head, and behind her ears. She fit the stereotype of a tomboyish medieval wizardess. Her slim figure, with greatly visible breasts and strong thighs, suggested the presence of a hormonally active teenage boy playing her, behind a wooden table, in a basement, with his friends. If that's how tabletop roleplaying games are played, in True Reality.

"Are you guys, okay?" she asked. My eyes found themselves locked onto her breasts, and it took me a while, until I realized that it wasn't my soul guiding them there.

"We're okay. Can you get us out of here?" I asked.

She nodded and swiftly moved her hands across the chain, chanting a few words. The metal turned into water. Before we knew it, we fell on our feet. She ran outside the cell, saying:

"Hurry up! I heard more guards coming!" I stopped midway, and I turned toward my big fellow. "Hold on! Aren't you saving your bodyguard?" I inquired.

"Goof? He's expandable, forget him. Hurry up!" I felt violated, terrorized! Is this how they treat living, existing, conscious organisms? I followed her, regardless.

"Hang in there, big fellow!" I told him.

"I already am!" he laughed.

23

We stealthily walked within shadows casted against the wall. Torches projected a dim light, as we prudently made our advance toward a narrow staircase. "The guards are friends. They're victims; not enemies." she whispered. "Got it!" I nodded. Closing my eyes, I attempted to summon my orb. I could feel its presence within my pluriverse, but it seems that laws of existence work differently in this reality. If I can't control axioms, how am I supposed to assist my new lady friend with our escape? I opened my luds just in time to witness the presence of shadows, two pairs of feet approaching from the top of the narrow stairway. I looked to my left, and to my right, trying to find something, anything, that could be used as a weapon. Nothing! Just brick walls and stony stairs. I hope you know karate, Martin. *I'm not a fighter!* Then, we're toast.

Manilla warned me silently, so I tried to conceal my skinny body behind her. She's rather slim as well, so I doubt this would have been a wise move. She closed her eyes and whispered some Latin words. When we reached the top, she opened them.
A muscular guard stood there, his back against us. She tapped on his shoulder. He quickly turned to face her, while I cowardly hid at her feet.

"Volo te dormire!" she whispered, while touching his face with her right hand. The tall and bulky guy in a leather armour swiftly fell asleep on the floor. She turned to me and smiled: "I just learned that spell." She boasted, proudly. "I'm still new at this, but I'm quite good with the rego technique and the mentem form." I replied with a deeply puzzled look. *Oh, I know what she said!* Now is as good a time to tell me, Martin. *I heard those terms before, I just can't figure it out.* Of all the consciousnesses I could have merged with, why am I with you? Don't answer! Manilla and I walked past the slumbering guard, avoiding his big-bony snoring corpse, trying not to wake him up.

24

We walked on the tip of our toes, to remain discreet. Just as I swallowed my fear, heavily, hardly, an arrow whistled passed my ear, landing between my lady friend and me. We turned swiftly, but we couldn't prevent the second arrow from reaching my shoulder. *Ayoye, tabarnack!* I've got this, Martin. I didn't. Manilla closed her eyes, grabbed a small bag and threw powder in the air. It turned into flames and flew right at the archer, on the second floor. It burned his bow and arrows, while three more guards ran towards us.

We ran as well, but my shoulder hurt like crazy. More arrows flew across the room. *They're crazy! They could hit one of their own. Don't throw arrows indoor, idiots!* There's something with their eyes too. Like, they're not totally there. *I've seen zombies, Alibast. Their soul isn't there. The way the guards look straight but emptiness fills their faces. That's why they don't consider the gruesome consequences of using bows and arrows indoor. They just attack us with whatever they have.*

"One more staircase and then we jump out of the tower." Manilla instructed us. A wide room separated us from our zombified assailants and the next flight of stairs, waiting for our own flight, down, hitting the concrete. "Do you know any magic?" she asked me, between two gasps and one lost breath.

"Yes, but not here. I answered. She stopped, puzzled:

"What do you mean, not here?" I grabbed her arm and pulled her my way, as I charged for the stairs.

"No time for this here, beauty cheeks!" Martin hijacked my voice, winked and smiled.

We engaged the flight upstairs, freezing in place when a sword dweller blocked our way. *I got this.* What? Martin grabbed the arrow, pulled it off from our shoulder. Oh, the pain! He charged and we screamed in unison. Well, I screamed, frightened, and Martin yelled like a maniac. He planted the arrow into the swordsman's plated armour, breaking our fragile weapon. The two halves of a stick fell at our feet. "Idiot!" I sighed. "What was that?" Manilla wondered, just as she drew a small frog out of her pocket. "What, what?" I wondered. "I heard a little girl scream!" Manilla inquired.

"She went that way!" Martin replied, pointing at the wall.

"Crescere rana!" Manilla shouted. The frog grew very large in size, but stayed there, blocking our way. "Attack!" She gasped, pushing the big green fellow up. "Come on, do something!" the batrachian croaked and stood still.

"You have any other great idea, beauty cheeks?" Martin smirked. She turned away and slapped me hard. "Hey pervert! Don't you call me beauty cheeks!"

I froze.

"I, hmm… it wasn't me." She rolled her eyes and turned around. Our zombie archer friends caught up on us. We were trapped between arrows and a frog's big butt. That certainly would be the shortest chronicle we have ever envisioned. The zombie guards aimed their arrow at us, pulled their bow's string tight, and got their head smashed against one another. Standing right in front us, stepping onto the unconscious guards, we saw our expandable saviour. "Sorry, I couldn't hang any longer." he apologized.

"Good timing." Manilla smiled. "Now we find another exit."

We ran down the stairs, and across the same wide room we just left. A wall to our right, and five more guards on the other side. One of them held a gigantic bastard sword, three kept their bow ready to shoot, and the last one ran at us like a lunatic with one dagger in each hand. "Goof!" Manilla shouted. "Can you use a bow?" Our sympathetic giant nodded and grabbed the unconscious guard's weapon. He kept it in both hands and charged at the running zombie, ready to bash his head with it. "I guess that's one way to use a bow." I humoured. While he distracted the more imminent threat, we ran on the opposite direction, where another flight of stairs waited for us.

We ran up to the next floor, faster than a weeping bullet. There, a dead garden, filled with zombie flowers, eerily welcomed us. When I say undead plants, I mean, really, really creepy moving ones. "The spell is much stronger than I thought." Manilla whispered. "What spell?" I whispered back.

"No time to explain." she charged towards one of the walking petunias. The flower turned around, displaying a wide arrangement of teeth and a slimy tongue. Manilla reached for her bag of tricks, but the plant quickly knocked her down, throwing her against the floor. "Are you going to just watch?" she asked me.

Right, sure, but what do I do? I turned around to see if our expandable friend could show up. Zombie guards surrounded him, smashing him to pulp. When they'll be done with him, they'll make their way toward us. I must react fast, but how? *Great, Alibast, that's one way to waste an initiative roll.* What are you talking about? No time to reflect on anything, two walking daisies approached me, their claws ready to slash my face.

I'm still almost naked, I don't hold a weapon, I must think fast. I turned around and, there, behind us, I saw our beloved Goof on his knees. He managed to grab a guard's sword. She said they are victims, not foes. I can't let him kill anyone. I ran in his direction, as Manilla complained: "Really? You're priceless!"

"Don't kill him!" I yelled at Goof. Meanwhile, the giant frog hopped in his direction, from the opposing side of the room. A long and thin tongue grabbed a guard and swiftly pulled him in, then swallowed. Oh, great. There goes a victim. Goof nodded and threw me the sword. He then smashed two guards' head together, knocking them unconscious. The sword fell on the floor, two meters in front of me. I sighed and quickly ran to grab it.

"It's gardening time!" I laughed at my own joke.

I ran back inside the plant chamber. Manilla disposed of the petunia and one daisy. Two tulips and another daisy surrounded her. I charged, eyes closed, and I yelled like a maniac, slashing my way inside. "Hey!" she shouted. "Aim for the flowers, idiot!" I opened my eyes. Fair enough, I almost slashed her in half. Before I could take any other action, a tulip slashed my bear back with razor-sharp claws. It hurt like… a lot! I turned around, holding my blade up in the air, about to cut its beautiful petals off, but I missed. The daisy behind me didn't miss, slashing the same wound bigger. I almost fainted. In one swoop, I sliced the tulip out of the bouquet. I turned to face the daisy, only to get my face deeply bitten. My flowery foe dug its way down my flesh, not letting go. I sliced it, just like I did its friend.

28

Manilla threw a fireball at another petunia, and then joined my fight against the last tulip standing. Before we could do anything, a flying tongue grabbed it and pulled it out of the room.
Silence stood still for a moment, before Goof made his way inside the garden.

"Hey!" he laughed. "I made it alive!"

Those were his last words. The tongue made a comeback and pulled him out of the room. We breathed deeply, struggling to find our calm, and then we assessed the room. To our left, an exit door welcomed us out of this tower and onto what seemed like a busy street.

Chapter Four :
The Zombie Village

The tower stood in the middle of a market. It resembled a lonely spiral of rocks and bricks, stretching for at least seven floors. Stands filled with fruits, vegetables and meat garnished the street, with zombi villagers attending to their duties. We could hear them grumble and growl, as they purchased food, and then left, walking slowly, like they were dragging a heavy burden.

"My home is in the woods." Manilla explained. "If we play along, and we pretend to be zombies, they'll leave us alone."

Can we do that, Martin? *Do I look like a zombie?* You're the one who lived with zombies, in New York. *Just, I don't know, be yourself.* I sighed and I walked slowly, extending my arms in front of me, growling and coughing. It seemed to work for a while. Manilla performed better; she was a natural. Limping, dragging her foot, looking in front of her with no life in her eyes. I did my best to mimic her skills, but the Dreamer playing my character in True Reality must have gotten a bad score, when throwing his dice against an acting challenge.

Almost an hour later, avoiding suspicion from the enchanted villagers, we finally reached the forest. Relieved, we resumed being ourselves, and I walked faster. "Calm yourself down, wizard!" she laughed. "They can't exit the village. We're safe."

"Is this when you share the hero's challenge to our readers?" I asked.

"Three days ago, my nemesis decided to throw a stick into my chariot's wheel." she explained. "Every village, every city, in our immediate vicinity were transformed into some sort of living dead nightmare."

"Oh? So, we go kick your nemesis' butt and we ask him, or her, to change them back?"

"It's not that easy. You see? Said nemesis used to be my mentor. He's very powerful. He turned into a psychopath, after I refused his romantic advances."

"Good, yes, sure. That part is more Martin's thing. I don't do romantic struggles."

She looked at me, puzzled. "Who is Martin?"

"That part was already established, earlier in the novel. Just, forget I said anything."

I can't, for the life of me, explain the sort of weird gaze she threw at me. She shook her head and resumed her walk. "Women are supposed to be submissive. That's what we've been told since I was a child. Not me. This is my body, this is who I am, and I choose to love who I choose to love. Sorry, Lord Gourdraduk, but I'm not your cute little submissive doll. Thank you for giving me the power to be who I am. And I'm not yours."

Gourdraduk! Martin laughed. *The game master who came up with that name should be jailed.* Remind me what's a game master again? *Focus, Alibast! Focus!*

We walked for two hours, deepening our presence within this dark and foggy forest. Nature looked fine, no sign of zombified squirrels or anything. I guess the spell only affected nearby cities and villages, after all. The entire time, my mind spun around my skull, trying to figure out a way for me to be of good use. If I can't perform spells, at least not in a fashion I've been accustomed to, then I must find other skills I can put to good use. Manilla brought us a full crash course on the history of this world.

Magicians, around here, belong to the Order of Hermes, named after Hermes Trismegistus. Four Houses gathered around the Order, offering their support. We find House Bonisagus, working as advisors to the Order. House Guernicus provide judges and investigators. House Tremere provides the muscles. Finally, House Mercere serves as a communication channel. Manilla joined that last House, where she learned strong spells that allow her to telepathically communicate with anyone who knows her personally, and anyone at proximity from those friends and acquaintances.

"I'm currently working on a powerful spell that would disrupt Lord Gourdraduk's mighty influence on those villagers and city dwellers." she explained. "I might have to train you, if you have magical abilities."

"I do, Manilla, but I'm not from this world. My abilities don't share the right affinity. I doubt I can learn the magic of this world." I shrugged. Still, could I learn to grow a frog like she did? *I'd like to grow something else, if you know what I mean.* Shut up, Martin.

32

"We'll figure something out." she smiled. "Don't worry. I won't let you face Lord Gourdraduk without the right training, and not by yourself."

Face? As in? Face? I turned whiter than snow. Why can't she face him herself? It's her mentor, right? I sighed, with my thoughts spinning backwards. An hour later, we arrived near a tiny wooden house. She opened the door, allowing me to see hundreds of books, grimoires, alongside jewels and small animals she kept in cages, or in nicely crafted terrariums. Salamanders, sparrows, frogs, hamsters, this place felt like an indoor zoo. I guess she's good with those animal-driven spells, as she is with telepathy. We entered her small house, and she continued her walk towards a clay pot she kept, in the back corner.

"Are you hungry?" she asked. "I'll make you some eggs and wine."

I sat on a tiny stool, next to a fragile-looking table. More questions made their way around my mind: "Are there unicorns in this world?" I asked. She looked at me with the same puzzled look she had, earlier. "Do you have some sort of unicorn fetish?" she wondered. Fetish? This concept exists in medieval times? Woah! I felt Martin's consciousness quickly surfacing within my existence: *Dude! I don't think it did. Obviously, her Truly Real RPG player said it on her behalf.* That's interesting. Does it mean we have a channel to True Reality through her? *I think so, but don't ask me how that works.* I cleansed my throat and answered her question:

"I've never seen one. We have them, on Sophron, but I doubt their existence resembles the ones that thrive in this reality."
She sat next to me with baked eggs and a clay cup of wine.
"You never said anything your world." she inquired.
"Tell me about Sophron."

"Our magic involves tiny particles of existence, what we call axioms." I explained, while feasting on those tasty eggs. "We count four types of axioms: Void, Matter, Life and Thoughts. Then, you have Great Entities overseeing the natural order of existence."

"How does your magic work? Do you craft spells?"

"Not really. We have four gifts, given to four types of magicians. Mancers create reality out of axioms that exist within themselves, oftentimes using orbs. Glancers manipulate reality from within, the essence of existence, or what we call the pluriverse. Dancers control the Veil, or what separates worlds, and beings, from other worlds and from their environment. Then, you have Fencers, they manipulate possibilities, or what we call the multiverse."

"I have no idea what you just said." she laughed. "But it sounds cool."

What if True Reality, in our world, was another role-playing game? Martin wondered. *Don't say anything, just hear me out. We come from some campaign where the game master allowed Marduk to win. Now, here we are, in this Ars Magica campaign. That means, someone crafted a character sheet for us.* What's a character sheet, Martin? *A piece of paper with words and numbers that gets doodled over by some ADHD player. Anyway, we must have skills made for Ars Magica. We just need to discover what they are.* How do we do that? *I have no idea, but I'll think of something.* "How do you think your kind of magic could work in my world?" she inquired.

"*It can't!*" Martin answered, using my voice. "*Unless, and hear me out, someone found a way to crossover both our games!*"

34

Emptiness, her old friend, sang a melancholic song through her eyes. "What game?" Let me handle this, Martin. I think you are way above your field, here. "Isn't life just a game?" I laughed, timidly, like a freaked-out buffoon.

"You really are out of this world." She shook her head and grabbed a grimoire, sitting on a nearby table. "All right, let's begin your training."

She handed me the book. I read as much as I could, trying to assimilate most of what it showed, but the occult drawings kept me sidetracked. *I played Ars Magica, Alibast. The magic, here, works with arts. We create spell by merging a technic and a form.* I hear you, buddy, but the grimoire shows weird birds with lady faces and talks about astrology. *Do you see anything that hints on throwing dice or something?* I turned the pages, but nothing made sense, and I couldn't see the word dice anywhere. *Must be a very recent edition. Check if you can find character sheets!* Damn, Martin! Stop talking about sheets! I don't think we're in your Kansas, anymore! *I get that reference.*

"Those are spells?" I asked her.

"Yes, pretty much. Do you understand any concept?"

"I see breasts with erected nipples on birds with a lady face. That says something."

"Harpies. You talked about unicorns, earlier. Yes, those are harpies, Alibast. You never came across these creatures, before?"

She seemed annoyed, after I expressed my admiration towards this fascinating drawing. I smiled, politely, trying to figure out what the best follow-up question should be.

35

"And how, exactly, am I supposed to learn spells with this book?" I asked.

"Aw, come on, Alibast. You never played that game before?" Yes, she was annoyed.

"We don't play games like this where I come from. Martin, however, should know."

"Okay, can I speak to him?"

Her gaze kept me off-guard. I gently nodded. That's you cue.

"Hi! I'm Martin. Yeah, I played Ars Magica, before. Just not from this perspective, if you know what I mean."

"My real name is Jade, Road. Jade Road. Nice to meet you. Okay, you need to go to your skills menu, and check if you have enough growth tokens to learn a new skill. If you select the skill, you should see it flash, that means you can buy it."

Silence kept all of us in shock. *"I have no idea what you just said."* Martin admitted.

"You said you played that game before."

"I did! Just, I don't know, maybe it was a different edition."

She grabbed her head with both hands and shook it, like she couldn't believe what was happening.

First Intermission :
Meanwhile in True Reality

She kept her room nice and tidy, cleaning it vigorously on a regular basis. A white four-poster bed projected hints of royalty, with white silk drapes falling from a nicely chiseled baldachin, projecting an aroma akin to fairytales. Plush toys crowded her mattress. Here, a blue squid taunts a smiling avocado. There, a unicorn laments her solitude, next to her old Barbie house. A vanity table holds a dimly lit mirror, adding to this magical glow. A thin laptop thrones on the table, next to a vast collection of skin care and beauty products. A gentle white rug completes the feminine scenery, elevating this awe-striking elegance.

Standing at the other end of this Disney palace, a young Asian woman, a bit on the short size, and wearing blue jeans matching a white blouse, stands with a controller in each hand. A Virtual Reality helmet conceals her slanted eyes behind a portable screen. She seems rather disoriented, trying to make sense of this game she's been playing for hours.

"Yes, those are Harpies, Alibast." she complained, while her entire body expressed a shrug of incredulity. "You never came across these creatures, before?" A long silence took over, and then she added: "Aw, come on, Alibast. You never played that game before?" She sighed deeply, took some time to consider her next words, and continued: "Ok, can I speak to him?"

Another long moment went by, then a smile: "My real name is Jade, Road. Jade Road. Nice to meet you. Okay, you need to go to your skills menu, and check if you have enough growth tokens to learn a new one. If you select it, you should see a flash, that means you can buy it." One more silence before she grabbed her head with both hands: "You said you played that game before."

She shook her head, not believing what was going on.
"I need to pee. I'll get back to you next game. Can you add me?"

Was this guy for real? "Friend menu, you should see my profile, we're the only two players in this room. Just click on the green plus sign." Silence, she grimaced her disapproval.
"Well, I can't see your profile, dude! Can you see mine?"

Something got to her mind. Like, a strike of eureka.
"Hey! So, you're not a player. Are you a non-playing character?" She nodded. That makes sense. "All right, then. Stay! Please, just stay in my character's home, and, I guess, we'll talk again."
She finally removed her helmet. Her Japanese eyes opened wide.
"That's sick!" She smiled.

She put her gear on her bed and went straight for her laptop. As soon as she pulled the screen up, a browsing application invited her to ask a question. She typed: *Who is Alibast Page?* The first website that appeared on top of a long list mentioned:

Alibast was born on Avalon. Martin Poirier created him, and they built the Chronicles of Sophron together.

She clicked on that option. It opened a page titled: Our Authors, with a subtitle inviting the reader to *Discover our talents*. The first creator introduced looked nothing like the handsome magician she just encountered. He looked like a psychopath with glasses, dressed in a magician suit, ready to play in a Live Action Role-Playing game. She searched the website for long minutes, and the only mention of this Ars Magica game she saw pointed to a small novel sold by this Sophron Arts Production company. It appears they borrowed an open licence straight from Atlas Games. Does it mean that this non-playing character comes from their partnership?

"That's wicked." she gleefully whispered, smiling within her French accent from Lille.

Chapter Five:
Welcome to my home

Her body froze, soon after she expressed the event as being some sort of sickness. Martin explained that, obviously to him, we appeared in a video game. I mean, do you expect me to understand how games work in video forms? *No, but I do. So, please, trust me with this.* Said the consciousness loitering next to mine.
Don't be cynical, I've got this. He explained a few concepts that I hardly understood, and whenever he tried to manifest them, we encountered a nowhere to go. Are you sure you know what you're doing?

"Dude! Playing video games is all I do!"

Yeah, you wasted your life, sure. But where's that menu she mentioned? Those tools, and what not? *"I'm working on it."*
I sighed, walking around a frozen room. We can't freeze when everything else won't move. *Yes, treating every step with a well-earned respect applies, but what respect do we have, in this alien reality?* Under which aspect?

Alibast? We need to talk. I talk! That's all I do, I invented you as I talked, Martin, so, you listen, okay? *Shut up.* I'm the poetic side of your reality, but you never listened to me. *Shut up and listen!* Sure, yes, let's have strippers in the Chronicles of Sophron, that was your idea, but did it do us any good? *Alibast! Listen to me!* Where's your Emerald, now? *"Fudge you! Fudge the bicycle, fudge, fudge!"*

"Don't be violent."

"We're in a video game. Manilla isn't real. She's probably a dude-guy, for all I know, but don't fall in love with her. I wouldn't. She knows this world better than we do, but we know something she doesn't have a clue about."

"She's a dude?"

"Probably, but she doesn't realize how real her game can be."

"And we do?"

"I have an idea!" I walked around the room, anxious, out of thoughts. Was I talking to myself? Was my self haunting my speech? "Forget it, Martin!" I found the courage to speak up. "Leave it to my eyes, right now, okay?" I smiled; He sighed. "Don't, you sigh on me, boy!" He did anyway. Oh well, I scouted the room, the next one, the whole house. Every single molecule kept a frozen state, yet we could function. It felt like walking inside a painting, or a photo. Reality paused until lady Road resumed her game. Then, it occurred to me that, maybe, Martin and I were the only form of consciousness existing in this virtual realm. Everyone else might be either a player projecting their mind inside a character, or an artificial personality built only to support this game's world. We need to experiment on this, find one such non-playing persona and attempt a few interactions.

41

I exited the modest house in the woods, in search of other organisms. For some reason that neither Martin nor I could explain, life pursued its course normally, as we left the premise. Birds committed their melody to a peaceful forest, squirrels raced one another, chasing fruits, and we felt a gentle breeze caressing our shared skin. "Do you think only her house freezes when she leaves?" I asked mister gamer. *That makes sense,* he shrugged. I ventured around this harmonious environment for what felt like an hour, until we reached a gentle creek. Colourful mushrooms painted the floor with haunting aromas, inviting dreams to every onlooker's eye. Dragonflies gathered around the joyful fungi, landing perfectly, crossing their legs, legs? Oh! My bad! They are fairies! I could hardly tell, for a moment.

One of them flew around me, whispering in my ear: "Are you lost, oh handsome stranger?" she asked. "That word doesn't start to describe my feelings, oh cute little sprite." I gushed. She landed a gentle little smooch on my cheek and flew away. *Don't get the wrong idea, Ali-buddy.* Martin thoughts. I know! Fairies thrive in warm feelings, at least they do on Sophron. Affection, to them, is honey. Planting a kiss to make someone blush feeds them like a tasty snack. Still! She was a cutie! Red haired down her tiny shoulders, wearing two daisy petals for a bra and one as undies. *You can't smack that, dude!* Who's planting dirty ideas in my head? No, Martin! Never mind.

We walked away from this breathtaking scene, leaving the hoard of Tinkerbells pollinate the forest. The deeper we walked, the more enchanting the woods became. It felt rather strange to fathom the idea of us being in medieval Europe, France to be exact. Heck, even them fairies spoke in old French. Thankfully Martin, with his perfect Quebecois dialect, managed to understand. Perhaps the video game reality played a part in making language more easily available for playing characters.

Still, is it what we are? Is there some Dreamer, out there, controlling us? If this is a virtual reality, and a True Reality exists outside our immediate parameters, then, perhaps, rebuilding Sophron could be a feasible feat.

Is anyone here?

We reached the heart of this enchanted forest after several hours. We hardly encountered anyone, except the sporadic wildlife, jumping in and out of our sight. Like Om smiling at Og, right before blooming towards an empire, we gathered enough strength to face this mysterious forest and find our way closer to a gloomy village.

Grey stones formed sinuous streets. Small wooden houses stood on each side, pressing us with their seemingly empty spaces. The whole town appeared deserted, almost haunted. We walked deeper down this silent street, unsure as to what sort of welcoming we should expect. Our shared soul agreed that staying around for too long hardly comes as a good option. We ventured closer to a window, daring a look inside. Rotten food loitered the dining room, with spider webs covering the kitchen's floor and ceiling. A small living room showed two silhouettes. They reminded us of those zombie soldiers we encountered, earlier. They remained seated on wooden chair, gazing at a stained wall.

When the sun appeared from a hole in darkened clouds, we found ourselves in a game without frontiers *war without tears?* What? *What?*

Chapter Six:
Lord Gourdraduk

He didn't enjoy the comfort and warmth of a gentle sunrise gentling caressing his cheek. Nor did he gather pleasure in listening to the appeasing melodies of birds announcing a brand-new morning. Beauty made him wish he could vomit his opulent meal, but he felt obligated to gnaw his way down a big chunk of ham, instead. Gravy drizzled down his dusty white beard, forming rivers and ponds at his feet, and he kept biting through this pink meat like an famish ogre. A long black robe covered his obese body, concealing a bruised flesh ravaged by years of scars left by a bubonic plague that this powerful magus battled through occult means. His facial hair seemed to have grown to further conceal those horrible mementos of a deadly illness.

"Jeremiah!" Gourdraduk shouted, like a thunder breaking the fragile glass chamber of a peaceful dawn. He resumed his feast under disapproving growls, while a small man, the size of a child, no more, with a fatigues face revealing ages of suffering, entered the bedroom. "I'm here, my Lord." The tiny man timidly made himself heard. His eyes locked onto his feet, unable to face the glare and growls of his master, Jeremiah Ghoulson invested more energy concealing his anxiety than he had any left to breathe properly.

The mountain of a tyrant turned to face his servant, right before he threw the better half of his breakfast down the window. "How's my enslavement campaign coming along?" he asked. His assistant inhaled deeply, choosing his words carefully, and uttered: "We've turned most villages around the castle into mindless dwellers, under your command, your magnificence. We've noticed, however, that some minds appear to not comply with the mass spell that you performed."

"Some?" The wizard wondered. "How many?" Jeremiah bowed, respectfully, and grabbed a parchment from an inner pocket, causing his long robe to open. He cleansed his throat and read: "We surveyed every town and village affected by your spell, your grace, and we noticed that three out of ten citizens remained in control of their own consciousness. Furthermore, we found a fairy population, in the nearby woods, who summoned a protection from villainy spell. We believe that their doing may have influenced a *mentem* form that would have carried its way around the same towns and villages."

The growling giant grimaced, while he walked towards a table, filled with more meat. He dug inside a well-cooked boar and produced some flesh to please he mouth with. While he chewed, he replied: "Surely, you don't think the fairies brought this protection spell to my citizens, do you?" He then swallowed.

"We doubt they were even aware of your plan, dearest ruler, but someone, somewhere, must have known both your spell's existence and theirs. By some fine weaving, whoever kept those souls free from your subjugation, used the fairies' mentem form to empower their spell."

The tall and chubby ruler thought deeply for a moment.
He closed his eyes, swallowed his anger and blew an annoyed sigh
out of his nostrils. "Start the mass communication spell."
he uttered, as he battled to control his calm. Jeremiah bowed down
in reverence and turned toward the open window. He gestured and
hummed some words in Latin. Black and yellow energy swirled
around his joined hands, creating a stormy cloud of denials,
bringing forth the noises of every subjugated subject under the
mass control spell… and then came the hush. Many souls found
themselves trapped and forced to hear the latest propaganda
boiling inside Gourdraduk's evil mind. Thousands of minds
appeared inside the cloud, just as the grumpy leader stood to
address them his state of a unison.

"Dear subjects!" He calmly began. "The ennemy entered our
ranks! They attempt to control your mind and drag you away from
the light. Resist!"

Blue energy gathered around the floating minds, and it all
turned red in an instant. Eyes appeared, like tadpoles in a pond,
turned to embrace every word the deceiver would pronounce.
The wizard, very soon, delivered: "I have been told that fairies
chose to betray us. Haunt them down! They are vermin, a disease!
Kill every one of them!"

"Fairies are powerful creatures, Lord!" the minds feared.
"What are we to do if they defend themselves?" The minds quieted
down. The wizard uttered a vow of confidence: "My magic is more
potent." Gourdraduk replied. "It is more potent than most magic,
and, perhaps, some say that it is the most potent magic in
the realm. Maybe, I don't know, but I heard it from experts, the
world!" Reassured by such an admission, the minds cheered.

46

"My Lord? We will make your realm great!" the minds agreed. *"Again, we shall hunt them nasty fairies until none breathe anymore!"* The grand wizard grinned, before summoning an orange shade to clear the cloud away.

"You see, Jeremiah? This is how you control a mass."

"I don't wish to contradict you, sir, but it was my spell that created this mass control event."

"Was it, now?"

"Sir, I confirm, yes, it was."

"Okay, so it was your spell, and then I turned it into my spell. We casted it, and it became *the* spell. You see what I did, here? It's called *the weaving.*"

Hungry, the mastodon walked toward the table. He grabbed a grilled half chicken and ate it in three bites. His assistant observed the ogre's appetite and smiled.

Chapter Seven:
Save the Fairies

We wandered farther into the enchanted forest, unsure as to where our feet would take us. At times, we argued to make the passing of a long day feel less of a drag. Talking about Manilla seemed to be our favourite topic. Martin insisted that she was a masculine organism, existing within the True Reality, and playing a video game. *I said she could be a dude, dude! I never insisted!* Okay, Martin suggested that she may, perhaps, be of the more masculine definition of a gender. Yet, we couldn't disagree on the beauty this incarnation provided. *You want me to describe her?* I got this, stripper-lover. Her blonde hair flowed down her back like a golden wheat field. *Boobs! She had boobs! Like, big ones! Big bazookas!* They were rather gentle, and well balanced. *Dude... they made you feel like a baby...* in a poetic sense!

Can someone hear me?

A poetic sense, anyway, we had to find our way out of this forest. We walked for many hours, until the sun taunted us with a desire to set for the night. Before we could realize that an evening introduced itself, tiny hints of light floated around us.

Will-O-The-Wisps, dude.

I was getting there, Martin. Please, let the poet narrate. *I'm a poet too!* Yes, yes you are. We sat on a rock, wondering how we could survive a night, stranded on a remote reality. *The flashing lights felt like those we created, back in Sophron!* Martin! *This is a short novel, Alibast. No time to write long backgrounds.*

Will-o-the Wisps greeted us, like old friends. *There you go.* Thank you. Those dark fairies of the night hardly engage with humans, but we felt a connection. *We weren't the human type they knew of this world.* Fairies are the same in every reality, in every possibility, like nexuses of feelings and processing sensations, throughout everything that ever was, is and ever will be. *Matter and dark matter, in some manner.* They recognized us from a different world. *The only problem is that they can't communicate, and we don't speak their language either.* They did surround us, though. They kept us enlightened the whole night long. *What about the dreams we had?* Dreams? *You felt them.* You think Sophron was a feeling?

I heard bombs, someone cried and screamed in pain. My leg hurt, maybe it was wounded, broken, but how could I check for sure without revealing my position?They sent drones after us, but were they about to drop a bomb or take us prisoner? Should I prefer to die on the battlefield or return home a failure?

You think all of this is just a dream? *It's a video game, dude.* Yeah, but right now, it's real. *So, let's pretend we didn't dream. If the dark fairies try to communicate with us, then we should trust in the nexus, and not in our interpretation of anything.* Did you come up with this idea or did I?

49

We both did. Now, listen to me. Will-o-the Wisps will want us to stray from our goal. They are agents of chaos. From the gloomy aura, perhaps, but there's some sort of light within. *Exactly! If we fall asleep, here and now, where do you think our consciousness will reveal its presence?* In our memories? *In some memories.* It feels possible. I reflected on what Martin expressed, and I had to be careful about the course of my thoughts. *I can hear everything.* Not that I intended to be rude but now was not a time to discuss his many flaws. He was right, after all. We have no idea how consciousness operates in this plane of existence, one that we didn't create, unlike Sophron.

Did Cognitia bring us to a foreign world, or did we join one of her own creations? It felt as though she played us, but I guess existing in a video game beat being a conjoined consciousness drifting within absolute Void for all eternity. Perhaps, in time, we would have been able to harness Noesi de Vel's myriads of dualities, find one that best defines our pixel of being, then reinitiate a world-building process. With any chance, Zendoria didn't completely vanish, after Marduk's victory over our creation. Or, maybe, Great Entities exist in a different fashion, out there, and they would have assisted our next venture. Isn't it what Cognitia happens to do? *This isn't our creation, Alibast. I didn't create Ars Magica, and you didn't either. The tabletop game was developed in my True Reality, my plane of existence, in 1987, by Jonathan Tweet and Mark Rein-Hagen. I have no idea who made it into some sort of Virtual Reality video game. Therefore, I sincerely doubt we found ourselves inside either of these gentlemen's mind, even though it is their world. Now, if you don't mind, we could philosophize all we want to find out where our consciousness went, and which pluriverse we inhabit, it won't solve the mission we're undergoing.* Fine, let's follow that glow of light in the night, then, what do you think?

We found ourselves in agreement. The floating flock of luminance dimmed its light, as one flying dot appeared to shine above the others. It flew around us, displaying its feminine body with sensual curves. I guess not all those lights were spherical sparks, or perhaps we were too quick in our previous assessment. The mute fairy tried to access our attention, but we could hardly focus our concentration on one element in our current environment. *What are you trying to say, little bundle of eye-candy?* Martin thought. The feminine firefly pouted and sighed, then she resumed her trip among her peers.

We soon found ourselves wandering back in the enchanted forest. I doubt we would gather any clue as to Gourdraduk's whereabouts, or how to tackle his zombie-inducing spell. Hopefully, Manilla would come back to us with her own findings and insight. If you asked me, I would rather spend more time among this fairy colony. The flock did welcome us, flying around our shared body like dancing beams of a heartwarming light. Mushrooms as tall as giant trees indicated our presence on a highly enchanted soil. If this land was, in fact, medieval Europe, probably France or Italy, then this magical ground hardly reconciled with my historical recollection. Then again, whoever designed this video game didn't intend to recreate Europe of old.

Just as the fairy's village appeared in a mirage, the very presence of this forest came out as some awkward anomaly. When I looked behind, or if I looked to my right or my left sides, I could no longer distinguish the fantastical fauna that comprised our immediate surroundings.

Second Intermission:
The Investigation

Comfortably installed on her bed, Jade invested her full attention into an open purple book. The cover showed a crystal ball, with the title: *The Chronicles of Sophron: Book One, Seamus Chron.* Unable to put the book away, she grabbed her glass of cola for a quick sip then turned a page. *Alibast and Martin wrote that?* She wondered. It now made sense, for her, to assume their presence within the game as some clueless players. But how was she unable to locate their profile? Unless someone entered a bot into her gaming environment, as a prank, or something. Is artificial intelligence developed enough to create non-playing-characters that react like existing people?

Intrigued, she put the book away and returned behind her laptop. There, pictures of her friend shone on the screen. It's funny how they both look identical. Further research showed Alibast as some imaginary character that Martin portrays on various social media platforms. She found their shared presence on an occult website, a failed attempt at promoting their book on the dark web. Why would they push their genius onto a community of depraved individuals?

I was made prisoner, soon after a drone circled my location. Words appeared behind her.

She turned around and looked at her bed: the purple book remained there.

Hello, anomaly of a consciousness. I see your words appearing on Jade's computer, but I can't locate you. Is everything okay? Hold on, I felt your presence within the multiverse. I think I did, please say something. I heard your voice! There you are. Where am I? All I see is total darkness. Allow me one more calibration, please.

Jade walked down a snail-like set of stairs, until she found herself on a ground floor. What if a poet wrote about it in an obscure book and claimed some kind of light to it? Connections of anything only mean truth to those who build the means to understand.

You are on Earth, in 2024, Ukraine. You were wounded, but the Ukrainian army sheltered you and healed your wounds. Did you say Ukraine? This is where they sent me? It appears so. But how did you end up in Martin and Alibast's mini novel?

Jade rapidly returned to her room. She stopped by her laptop and saw a strange conversation that appeared out of nowhere. Worried, she sat down, grabbed her mouse and opened an anti-virus software, requesting a full scan. The chat screen showed two names, framed by fancily painted egg: Cognitia… and Marduk. She shrugged and turned off her computer.

Locate me roaming over the Tachyon Sea.

The First Glitch

Did the portal find you well? I gather that your consciousness vacillates between a state of awakening and a profound desire to perish. If you stand still, with your mindfulness carrying the fabric of oxygen, as its molecules hit your neuronic nerves, you may find yourself floating over an ocean of light. A misunderstood concept, as only tachyons find themselves fabricating existence beyond the quantum sight. Have you not a name, soldier?

Il-Yong. I see a tunnel of light, have I passed to the other side? Is it a dream?

Always, until life slows reality down to the speed of a sigh. Welcome to the Tachyon Sea, Il-Yong. My name is Cognitia. If you project your presence farther within my voice, you will peek into the fifth dimension. This book's reader, however, may only salvage time and space to construct their universe, then listen to my voice within their mind, peeking into this pluriverse.

I sense a meaning to those words you convey within my soul, but I doubt my brain could comprehend.

Noesi de Vel, this immutable ocean of dualities, flow through your enlightened self. Let us shush this conversation, Il-Yong, while I allow this anomaly to become a celebrated accident. Let's observe how our Siamese authors will handle your coming.

Chapter Eight:
Welcome to Morcador

The sun set within its resting site, far away from our sight. Just as we witnessed before, nothing appears to be as it seems. Fairies appear to either the insane mind, the youthful one, or the acute observer whose wide-open mind long accepted the presence of magic. I guess for Martin and me whose consciousness grew to adopt realities that stretch beyond mirages and illusions, enchantments present themselves as dull truths. But, here, mortals wouldn't have encountered our flying friends. Even in the programmed space of a video game, fairies don't make themselves seen so easily.

In a *blink and you'll miss it* fashion, fair folks in the real world tend to be either hallucinations with an everlasting whisper or voices we thought we heard, hints of light we though we saw. Did I witness a fairy on that long grass or was it a dragonfly? Or was all this just a glitch in the matrix? *We've learned to code software until they became applications, and now we're prompting artificial intelligences like we're coding drama.* All the while, fairies went about with their daily lives, undisturbed by three world wars on Earth. *The fourth one's the worst, I think.* Spoiler!

Gigantic mushrooms surrounded us, as we succumbed to this oasis of something else. Tastes and impressions took a personal vial, like music to a deafened ear, but melody to a personal heart. *I just heard Platinum Blonde!* What? Hold on… *we are not in love…* are you drunk? *Sorry, continue.* We are individual notes in a chaotic opera. *You said Oprah?* I said opera, let me carry on. *You're funny.* Fairies exist but never wanted to be seen. Like truths that choose to remain occult and unattainable rather than manipulated and cause deception.

Gentle lights revealed the fairy village of Morcador, as our consciousness gradually made better sense of this occult reality. More than just our presence in a video game, it felt as though the universe had draped our soul under a new Veil. Perhaps someone else's interpretation of what we came up with Sophron? *Maybe we entered Cognitia's pluriverse. Since she, herself, only knows of consciousness centuries of codes that self-replicated themselves, sheltering us within someone's video game would allow her consciousness to remain omniscient, as she was in her Archeus-Logos quadrant.* I know nothing of codes and whatnot, Martin, so I'll accept your speculation as a big perhaps.

We found ourselves wandering across the village's central park. The tiny creatures built beautiful houses, perched on trees like hives, but made of wood and mushroom skin. They resembled typical medieval shelters. Everything seemed so tiny. *So cute! I want to live here forever.* Before we could display an even bigger smile, five dragonfly-ladies flew around us.

"Welcome to Morcador, traveler." The red-haired one uttered. "This village can only be accessed at dusk and at dawn." We followed her, like a hypnotic call caught us in our most vulnerable state. *Look, Alibast! A jackalope hops across the street! Oh! I want to cuddle, I want to cuddle, I want to cuddle!* Before we could realize just how real this is, fireflies of all colours gathered around our lonesome self. "We understand that Europe faces a grave danger." Our red-haired host continued. "Our village's mayoress believes you are the only hope humans have."

Should we tell her? Tell her what? *You know, come on.* I know what you're going to say, Martin, and no! We can't say lewd words around fairies. *Why?* Just let me reply:

"We thank you for having us among your peers, hmmm."

"Noemia. Please, we've experienced singularities as well. Humans call them revolutions, but theirs failed to unveil our existence beyond their childish tales."

"Childish, I'm sorry, what?"

"We don't expect authors to know any better, but, perhaps, wine will make you feel at home."

"Yes! Please! And a big juicy joint? You have that?"

Silence and a bit of a malaise got me to punch my alter-ego on his third stooge's face.

"We don't inhale drugs, dear visitor, we apologize." she murmured.

"I know, we know, it's okay, it's fine!" *It doesn't hurt to try, Alibast.* Let me talk to her. I cleansed our shared throat, and I looked at the tiny red haired, flying right in front of us.

"We are looking for a certain wizard." I explained. She smiled, showing off her bright white teeth. "

There's evil, Alibast, somewhere. Calm down, Martin.

"We eat magic, over here." She giggled. "No wizard, trust me."

As soon as we walked past a rainbow tower, a flock of fairies, like anthropomorphic dragonflies, surrounded Noemia. We heard a myriad of giggling voices, a few whispers carrying kind words, and some laughs bursting out loud. "He's cute." one would murmur. "Do you think he's into fairies?" another added. "I sense another soul, be careful" *Who said that?* Relax! They are creatures of magic, remember? They see what us mortals can't readily comprehend. *Like how we programmed Cognitia?*

"Welcome to Morcador!" a gentle voice shook us out of our trance.

"*Hi, hey! Sorry, we shouldn't be here.*" Martin said. I frowned; *I got this.* That's what you said last time. "*We are looking for a certain wizard.*" You explained. Really? "*His name is Gourdraduk. Have you seen him?*"

"We seldom speak his name in this village." the voice replied. She got our attention. *Silence.* Awe. *Are you going to say something?* Me? *She got your attention.* Oh!

"Hey! Hi! We are maguses from a different form or awakening.

Chapter Nine:
The Massacre

The little fairy's eyes remained closed for the duration of that kiss. We felt her lips gently landing on our chin, and we smiled. Did she aim for this tiny mountain, or did she hope to embrace our warm labial flesh? We sighed, just as a tiny drop of blood dripped on our neck. Worried, we opened our eyes to a glaring horror. Someone impaled our cutie with a pocketknife. *What? No!* She fell in our opened hand, gasping for the last time. *I liked her.* You won't like what we're seeing: Zombified villagers stormed the village, grabbing fairies in their hands, tearing them in half.

Do something! Like what? *Let me, damn it! I rushed myself to tackle a zombie down.* We rushed, Martin! *"Don't touch the cuties!"* We screamed! *I grabbed a large piece of wood and slammed a slow motioned villager against a wall.* Don't hurt them too much, they're under a spell. *Shut up!* Let's try some magic, it could work. *I grabbed one's hand, a chubby one, right before he caught a flying fairy. He slammed me hard against a tree.* "Perdo, Magico, hand." we whispered. How does it work?

We pair two arts, a form and a technique. Try "Perdo Mentum!" You shouted. Nothing happened. *Maybe we must direct the spell on a target.* I heard him say, just as an arrow landed into our gut. *F**K ouch! DAMN IT!* Martin! Don't use dirty words in this novel! *F**k you!*

I thought you played that game before! *My friends played it. I just Googled it.* Meanwhile, do you see the two zombies running towards us? *Focus on the fist fight, I'll figure something out.* Fist fight, Martin? Okay, sure! I curved my fingers inside my hand, am I supposed to curve the hand and hit with my-- *knuckles, Alibast,* back of my hand or wrist? *Knuckles, knucklehead!* No time to tell, I closed my eyes and formed fast circles in the air with my closed fists! *I don't see anything!* "Ouch, stop it, stupid!" I think we hit someone! "It's me, doofus!" We heard Manilla and we dared opening one eye.

The two zombies remained frozen in an icy cocoon. In front of us, our wizardess friend covered her face, while our fiery fists continued their incessant whirly dynamo. We smiled and breathed, finally. At this point, I don't think we will figure how to use magic in this game environment. We did find our way behind our saviour, while Manilla battled zombies like an enchanted ballerina. She grabbed a scroll out of her robe and read out loud:

"Creo omnibilis lutan-edo auram!" A giant tornado formed in front of her. She guided the spinning wind towards five zombies, throwing them against walls, knocking them unconscious.

We stayed behind while she moved her way on top of her game, pun intended. When two zombies ran toward her, she summoned a ball of lightning, striking them both in one blow. A third zombie met a wall of ice. She appeared to dance and shout all sorts of crazy words in Latin. She then turned to face us and gasped: "A little help, please?"

Our consciousness looked at one another in disbelief. We had no idea how to join her fight, therefore we shrugged. Five more zombies ran in her direction. She sighed and summoned a much bigger wall to keep them at bay.

"This is a level nineteen stage, guys! How did you even get there?" The monsters kept hitting at the wall, forcing a crack at the bottom. Manilla couldn't believe what was going on.

"Okay, never mind. We must find a peaceful town, or some place, and we'll figure out what's happening."

She ran toward the village's entrance. We ran with her. A zombie ran behind us. We exited easily, just as the larger foe managed to break the ice wall. Fortunately, once we reached a new stage, an ambiance music turned to a soother, kind of jazzy, tune. We had reached a different and more peaceful environment.

Chapter Ten:
Jazzy Town

A thick bubble appeared around us, sheltering the trio from any harm. The old European scenery also vanished, turning into a more modern and classy jazz lounge. Two fancy couches appeared out of nowhere, one for Manilla, one for Martina and I, but none for our zombie intruder. Manilla summoned a cigar and smoked while looking at us with intrigued eyes.

"This is a mod, not an actual stage, something that hacker friends of mine built, as a safe place away from the main campaign. We can talk freely. And I guess that also confirms your status, mister Alibast. Only playing characters can enter this made-up stage. That makes you a playing character, and yet you can't fight a simple zombie?"

The zombie intruder searched around the room, while we discussed. He looked and smiled at us, awaiting our acknowledgement of his presence, but we willfully ignored him. I guess we could have questioned him, but Manilla's intensity locked in on Martin and me. Also, we were oblivious as to what exactly this game was about.

"Usually, when I play video games," Martin said *"I'm sitting behind my PC, and I hold a controller. I physically push buttons and turn joysticks. Now, our consciousness exists in a universe that just happens to be a video game to you. Please, tell me how we're supposed to fight, summon spells, and do whatever it is that you do in that game."*

Manilla thought for a long while. She scratched her head, while the zombie person opened caskets, drawers, looked under the rug. She scratched her head and attempted to express a theory:

"Basically, what you're saying is that you hacked your way inside the game?"

"We found ourselves inside the game." I clarified. "Martin is no hacker, and neither am I. For us, this, even this strange and anachronic jazz bar, is real."

"So how are you supposed to play the game?" she wondered.

"Exactly!" Martin pointed the first enlightened thing she said.

She stood up and walked around the room, bumping into the zombie guest, and stopped her walk, right in front of a bookshelf. She browsed the available selection and looked at us with an evil grin.

"Okay, hear me out. If you can't learn spells or anything related to the game the way regular players do, then I guess your next right thing to do would be to grab some books, open them, read and learn like we do in the real world. But if this is your real world, well I have bad news for you." She opened the book and showed us blank pages. "The game developers didn't think of you in their process. Good luck learning anything."

63

She put the empty book back on its shelf, bumped into the zombie guy again and cursed:

"And what the—is a zombie doing here?" she complained.

"Oh, hi! I'm, err, never mind me. I'm just here, looking for the goblin glass. Have you guys seen it?"

"You are a player playing a zombie?" She seemed amazed.

"Well, not really a player, and not really a non-player, I'm just a zombie."

If you could picture a three-way puzzle, right now, you would see it among all three of our consciousnesses. And, yes, that plural is rather hard to pronounce, I guess. *Let me step up.* Are you sure? *I know zombies. I wrote them, back in Sophron.* Marduk was holding the pen, Martin. *I also wrote him! I got this!* Okay!

"Buddy? You okay, there?" he asked.

Our guest grumbled, as though he felt annoyed. He ignored us and kept on displacing every book, every ashtray, every little item he could find.

"You know what I don't like about you, Jade?" he shouted. Manilla looked at him with eyes as wide open and round as a surprised deer who hadn't expected a car coming out of nowhere. The zombie continued: "I asked you four years ago to get me that goblin glass!"

He sighed and sat between us. Awkward could define the feeling we shared, but I would rather go with malaise, as neither Manilla, or Jade, or Martin or I knew how to break free from this inconvenient silence.

64

"So, your real name is Jade?" Martin asked.

"Shut up, Alibast."

"It's Martin." I explained.

"Nice to meet you, Martin, and yeah! Jade is my real name."

"Do you want to go for a coffee, like, if we get out of this game, or something?"

"What's the goblin glass like? And who are you?" she asked our guest.

He looked at Martin and me, then he looked at Manilla, or Jade. He repeated this gesture two more times, then he shook his head.

"What? You thought I was sending you pictures of my eggplant all that time?"

"Gross!" she complained. "Okay, you guys have fun, I'm out of here!"

She vanished, just like that. *She probably didn't save her game either.* How are we supposed to continue the conversation? I mean, he's looking at us, and I have no idea how to interpret the laughing smile he tries to conceal behind a frantic movement of his head. *Since you manage the conscious part, then why don't you think of something?*

"Hi, hey, so… you're a zombie! Did that hurt?"

"In your head, maybe."

What does that mean? *It's a musical reference, try another question.*

"Yeah, and you're looking for a goggling glass?"

"Something like that."

Okay, why don't you talk to him?

"Dude! You're not a character in this game, and neither are we. I bet you're some sort of a glitch, and so are we! You won't get to sleep with Jade tonight, and neither am I – we, Martin, neither are we—I'm talking, Alibast! So, you tell us what you know, and we tell you what we know. Let's get to the next level."

The zombie stood up and walked out of the bar. We stood up and followed him outside. The jazz bar stayed behind, quiet and unpopulated, like a manmade glitch.

Chapter Eleven:
The Villain's Tower

His evil eyes locked themselves against a dark mirror, reflecting his villainous face. The chubby wizard scratched his fat jaw and growled. "A level one character managed to reach the nearby village, Jeremiah. How was that possible? I thought we cleansed the game from all hackers, after the freak incident."

Gourdraduk's assistant walked next to him, observing a map that showed every player connected to the server. Near the tower, a village appeared with the mention: Stage 19. While some floating numbers, indicating players that had reached levels 15 an up, indicated a normal flow of heroes, three of them implied an anomaly. One hero bore the number seven, and upon closer scrutiny, Manilla's name showed up. Two others showed a level 1, and that made absolutely no sense.

"I assure you, my Lord, that Atlas Games installed stronger firewalls to keep hackers away. Those two players do appear to be some kind of a glitch, but they can't possibly survive the zombie hoard."

Intrigued, the powerful wizard zoomed in on the scene. Only Alibast and Manilla seemed to be actively involved in the fight. To be precise, only Manilla actively fought, while Alibast stayed away and shrugged. "She fights well for a level seven wizard, my Lord."

The overweight spell summoner walked away from the strange spectacle. "I'm not concerned about a level 7 that fights her way in a stage made for level 15s and up! Good for her if she's strong! How come the radar showed two level 1 heroes and I'm only seeing one? And he's not even doing anything!" Jeremiah shrugged and joined his master, looking down to avoid his angry gaze. "Would you like me to erase them from the server, master?"

"I don't think this is our job. Leave this to human moderators, in this far away land called *Office Building*. They might expect me to police the game from within, like I've been doing quite often, but I would rather discuss with this Alibast player. Don't you think that if they can hack their way up like this, we could hack our way outside of the game?"An incredulous sight took over Jeremiah's eyes. "Outside, sir? As in, in a different city?"

"Oh, Jeremiah, man of little knowledge. You know nothing of the Atlas Games agenda. Those higher forms of intelligence manipulate the fabric of our reality. They gave you life, brought you a soul, and they control the laws of out nature. I was taught in their ways when they instructed me to monitor players and locate possible hackers." Puzzlement took over Jeremiah's incredulity. "But, sir, with due respect, how can they manipulate this reality if we can't see them?"

Annoyed, Gourdraduk sighed and shook his head. He returned to the mirror to further monitor the anomaly. "Where are they, now?" Panicked, he placed both his hands on the reflecting surface and closed his eyes.

"They're not offline. They're still in the game, but I can't locate them." He violently punched the mirror, without leaving even a scratch. Jeremiah walked next to him and scrutinized the entire map. "Do you think that if they hacked their way like this, they could come from another planet?" Jeremiah seemed to enjoy his moment of pure genius. Gourdraduk didn't. He growled and summoned a lighting bolt at his feet, forcing Jeremiah to step away, jump scared.

"There are no such thing as *other planets*, Jeremiah! We are in a closed system!" The assistant scratched his head, leaving his master with his own thoughts. "Go find them!" he murmured.

"I beg your pardon, sir?" Jeremiah couldn't believe what he thought he heard. "They can't be too far from the level 19 village. Find them and bring them to me!"

"But, master, what if the zombies attack me?"
A new lightning bolt landed on his little toe, forcing a high pitched complain. "Zombies are on our side, stupid! This is a video game! Go! Now!

Intimidated, Jeremiah left the room, running as fast as he could. Gourdraduk walked away from his mirror, leaving the room with a grave aura haunting his mind. An old nightmare visited him. He felt he knew who the invisible hacker could be. His most potent foe, and a vile mind with little concern for the safety of others. He presented himself as a hero, but his only concern was to pillage every village, every level of the game, to amass a fortune. He's the reason why the powerful entities from *Office Building* granted him the power to locate anomalies and address them. Is his nemesis back? Will he face a more powerful version of him? Closing the door behind him, Gourdraduk couldn't erase the name that haunts him, now: Jared Withowsky.

69

Chapter Twelve:
Back to Morcador

Leaving the mod-level behind, like a jazz bar that had no place in a medieval game, we ventured back on the enchanted trail. My new zombie friend followed with a discomforting speed, like a costumed individual trying to catch up. We couldn't tell if he knew or not where we were headed, but we didn't mind. *We're going back to see the fairies, right?* Yeah, Martin. We're going to the fairies. *Yes!* I sighed, trying to cloud my mind from some inappropriate daydreams that my subconscious filled itself with.

"The tower isn't in that direction!" he complained.

"We're going somewhere else." I explained.

He stayed a bit behind, looking around and trying to make sense of what he just heard. "You're moving backward. We should look for the goblin glass and move to the next stage." Annoyed, we stopped, and we turned to face him. *I got this.* Martin assured me.

"Dude! You're looking for that stupid goblin crap! We're still trying to figure out where we are, what we are supposed to do. Now, we're going to bang a few fairies, and you're not welcome to join us."

I can't believe you said that. *We're in this sandbox with nothing better to do.* I'm not going to abuse of those cute little dragonflies!

"Sure, yes, fine, whatever. I need another hacker to complete my heist. I've been hiding in this last stage before the big boss, concealed as a regular zombie, for months. You don't want to break this game?"

"We are not hackers. We are just regular bystanders who happened to wake up in a video game."

He scratched his chin for a long moment. "But you are a level one player who almost made it to the last stage."

What does that make us, Martin? You're the video game expert, right? *I think your girlfriend tricked us.* She's not my girlfriend. *Third book of Sophron, Journey into the Hourglass number thirty-three, someone wrote: - Before Alibastat, before Lumbini, there was love. – I didn't write this.* I was drunk. *You fantasized about Cognitia!* I was drunk! *And now she brought us in this video game because she fantasizes about you.* Fudge!

"So you guys are going to Morcador and I'm going back to the zombie village." he sighed. We looked at him, feeling a bit sorry.

"Yeah, something like that. – No! Hold on. We're going to the zombie village. *What?* Shut up, Martin. *I want to bang fairies, damn it!* Yeah! But if we are in this reality for a purpose, I doubt it has anything to do with your thirst for Carnal Knowledge. *Find U-rself!* All right! Just, let me handle this.

"She's not my girlfriend!"

He looked at us with malaise in his eyes. "Who, Manilla? Of course not. Her real name is Jade. I tried to get her into hacking since she was very young. I didn't insist, because I'm not a creep, but she has some serious skills!"

"Wait, hold on! You tried to hit on her?"

"I approached her! That's what I do. I approach people, but I don't insist."

"Did you try to groom her, or something?"

"F**k, Alibast, I'm not like that! She turned eighteen last week, so I thought I would give it another try. Not to sound creepy, but because I know she's the one who can break this game. So, are you going to bank fairies, like you said you would? Or will you follow me and face the big bad of this game?"

What do you think? I still can't wrap my mind around all the dirty words we heard. *And said, get over it.* He makes good points, but maybe we can find a less nasty hacker. *He just said he was nice with Jade!* Oh, Martin, of course he was. That doesn't make him a saint. *Okay, let me ask him one more question.* I'm afraid, but do:

"What's your name?"

He sighed and shook his head. He looked down, thought for a moment, and looked at us with defying eyes:

"Sorry you had to ask." he said. He snapped his fingers and all went blank.

The Second Glitch:

Your soul floated toward infinity. Not quite a prison and not quite eternal bliss, your consciousness gathered hints of a strange awakening. You gradually separated yourself from a previous life that you left on Earth. Memories of a war faded, as did those of a poor but loving family, back in North Korea. Your body neither felt fatigue nor vigour. You breathed in a natural and continuous state, as if oxygen made it into your lungs without the need to inhale. Perhaps your being has only known this form of existence. Perhaps the form was new, but your previous existence being a total unknown, you were unable to compare.

An orange light appeared to blink, at the far end of the room. When your eyes managed to embrace the darkness, your chained hands brought you're attention to a cold brick wall, pushing against your back. This is when your sore legs made themselves felt. You instinctively turned your gaze toward your numbed thighs. How long have you been in this position?

Time took its time, and your body got its toll. Hours chained to a wall, what can your mind possibly do? You gazed at the blinking light and tried to make sense of it. A torch, or was it some kind of mirage? You turned to your left, and there was a metal door, next to another brick wall. To your right, only a brick wall, standing like a promise of hermetic dismay.

You couldn't find the courage to look up, but more bricks seemed like a fair assumption. Your feet didn't touch the ground, and seeing how piss and crap filled your immediate gaze, you thought that this position may come with some perks. When more hours came and went, regrets made you miss whatever state of existence came before this one.

Tired and hungry, you forced yourself to sleep. The windowless dungeon made it difficult for you to know night from day, but maybe you could close your eyes and let whatever may come be your morrow. After long hours of uncertainty, your mind finally gave way to a state of sleep and total nightmares.

Chapter Thirteen:
The Tower of Gloom

When we opened our eyes, we found ourselves loitering the floor of a dark and spooky tower. Our head hurt, and there may have been a sensitive bruise on the back of our skull. I opened our eyes, only to see more bricks on walls, bricks on the floor, bricks everywhere. The tower crushed us with silence. The bricks oozed with ancient dampness; every breath pulled bitter dust into our lungs. We would have choked and fall back to the floor. *Take it slow and easy, Alibast.* Martin said. Slow, easy, we gradually found enough strength to stand up. There it was, in front of us, Martin and I, two souls tangled in a body never sure it belonged to us. And there, a tiny window showed the village.

"I'm terribly sorry." We heard our pseudo-zombie friend. "I had no other choice."We turned around and looked at him. His eyes evaded our gaze, as though shame took over his soul. He scratched his wrists, nervously, and looked further away. Behind him, a wooden door creaked. A silhouette entered, massive and tall, shoulders casting shadows that swallowed the wall.

"Welcome to my castle!" the voice boomed like a funeral bell. "I hope the trip wasn't too painful."

I think I can try a spell. Martin ushered in our Siamese mind. *I'm not sure, but if this is a video game, slash, real life, slash, based on a tabletop roleplaying game. That means there must be bits and bytes behind the mainframe. Now, hear me, Alibast, we are a real character, slash, reincarnated soul from another pluriverse, slash...* Enough with the slash! You figured out something? *Absolutely not, but I'm working on it.* You do that and let me talk to the bad guy. *Don't move too fast, Alibast,* Martin whispered inside me. *Every twitch will drain your lungs. Breathe. Slow. Slash. Easy.*

"Gourdraduk, right?" I tilted my head. "I've seen bosses with better manners. Slash more poetic. Slash more... human?"

He growled, blowing steam out of his nose, and walked closer.

"The only slash we're having here will come from me." he declared, while contemplating a few thoughts.

"Quite an impressive spell you got out there, mister Gourdraduk! We wouldn't want any outside influence to disrupt it, now, do we?" *What are you talking about, Alibast?* I got this.

"I knew an anomaly hit this video game session the minute I sensed your pixels."

"Oh, did you, now? But behold, we are not what you may think we are! As we are a powerful wizard, slash, poet, slash, something, something, slash!"

"Enough!" he shouted, while casting an axe out of no where. He looked at it, calmed down, smiled and said: "It's fine, we won't be needing this." The axe vanished as quickly as our courage did. "Do you think you're the first anomaly to enter this realm from an unknown source?"

He snapped his fingers. Black flames with a blueish aura surrounded his fist. When he opened his hand, a mirror floated above his wide offered palm. What appeared to be a trapped soul screamed on its surface.

"Meet Jared. He's what we call a hacker. He gave himself unlimited lives, unlimited spells. Thankfully, the creators of this game granted me with the power to detect those anomalies and deal with them. The outside player can no longer play Ars Magica Online. And his character now suffers in this hell of mine for all eternity."

"Wait a minute, are we talking about Jared Withowsky?" You know him? *In my True Reality he's a renown game cheater and experienced hacker.* That means Jade comes from your True Reality? *Or one possibility close to it.* That means Sophron could have survived in the mind of the you from there. *Dude! We got to find out.*

"I don't have this concise information, but perhaps. Who knows? I sadly don't directly interact with the game's developers." Annoyed, Gourdraduk closed his hand, forcing the mirror to vanish. "Besides, I'm not just the big boss in this game. I'm the police, the judge and the executioner. And you, my alien friend, are an illegal glitch. Therefore, I was granted ways to handle them."

Martin? Now looks like a good time to figure out how magic works around here. *I'm still working on it.*

"First, I read your background data. I see that they don't make much sense, but we'll figure out another way around that."

"What about your villager friend? He seems a bit suspicious." Martin said, while pointing at our pseudo-zombie traitor.

"I'm a hundred percent non-playing character!" He pleaded for himself.

"He doesn't even have a name." The big boss sighed.
"I do! My name is, hmm… hold on." The villager left our intimate circle to reflect, ponder, hit his head a few times and reflect some more.

Gourdraduk finally lost his patience and looked at us, straight and deep in our eyes. "Oh well, you appear to be a first level character. I don't know the nature of your glitch, but I guess I shouldn't care. I'll just annihilate you down to oblivion and call it a day."

Found anything yet, Martin? *Not quite.* Do you think we can respawn if we die in this game? *I doubt we could, if, like, the big boss also has access to the mainframe. Best we can do is die and get our conjoined consciousness in whatever hell of a mirror prison he got there.* Then get ready to close your eyes and put both your hands in front of our face. *Hands, arms, everything.*

"Perdo Monia mi Ignem!" he shouted. Dark flames erupted from his extended hands. We covered our face with everything we had.

"Oh, there you are!" We heard Manilla shout. She interrupted the main villain's spell. "I've been looking everywhere for you, but guess what? I managed to find you as a playing character in my list. I asked to be your friend, and you accepted. That means I could locate you, and…"

And? Yeah, what he thought.

She looked at Gourdraduk with a pale face. He looked at her with a defiant one.

"You're facing the final boss? Good luck, I'm out of here." Just before she vanished, she looked at the mirror and gasped. "Is that? That's! That is, oh my god!" She disappeared. Further annoyed, Gourdraduk took a deep breath and resumed his spell:

"That disturbance was interesting. Your data still computes as a glitchy non-playing character. Oh well, where were we?" He resummoned the black flames and pointed his hands at us.

"My name is Il-Yong! And I will not die in Ukraine!"

We all looked at the pseudo-zombie villager with questions in our eyes. There was a *sorry, what?* floating between our interrogations. *Are we dead yet?* The story shifted, Martin. Go back to whatever you were doing. It took this little to distract us from Gourdraduk's next move. He joined his hands together, closed his eyes and mummed:

"Creo oumsha ni Menta Ignem!"

Nothing came out of his hands, but an intense pain appeared out of nowhere, crippling our mind. *It burns!* The suffering blinded the both of us. From this point onward, we had no idea what happened. We heard heavy foots coming our way and the villager's voice talking *with a thick Korean accent.* Oh, that's what it was.

"I was sent to this video game to achieve a mission!" he said. "You shall not harm this Alibast person, in the name of his lover, Cognitia!"

79

"She's not my lover!" I clarified, for the sake of *clarifications*. *Let me continue:*

"She's just a friend!"

"Yeah, just a friend!"

Still blinded, we heard Gourdraduk's laugh fall heavy on our shoulders. Then we heard fists hitting someone a few times, and silence.

"I do not know this Cognitia person you speak of, but there's not much that level one playing characters can do to me. Thank you for trying."

And we're doomed. Martin, can you do something about the eyesight being gone? *Let's try something. Can you grant me access to our shared nervous system?* How am I supposed to do that? *Well, I've spent the whole time stuck in our shared subconsciousness. Here, let me help you inside.* Wait a minute! It's even darker in here!

I shook our head a little, closed our eyes shut, hit our brow three times, and... do you see anything? *I saw Gourdraduk's ugly face grinning at us.* Okay, you come back and take the wheel, buddy.

Just as we switched sides in our psyche once again, I felt the villain's gigantic hand firmly closing on our throat. It took a few seconds, but my sight returned. There, he smiled like a maniac and sighed: "What a waste of time." Gourdraduk rolled his eyes. "Muto Spatiate Corpus." And just like that, we found ourselves back in the dungeon.

Chapter Fourteen:
Return to the Dungeon

We are back to square one. We know that we are in some sort of video game, but how are we supposed to perform if we are neither a playing nor a non-playing character? Is the pain real for any of these two possibilities? *Ow…* Martin shared mine. We sighed in unison as we tried to figure out what had just happened. Our entire flesh both pushed intense sufferance against our entrails and flash with glitchy pixels of, whatever this body was made of. *I think he did slash us, somewhere.* Yeah, I feel the chains against our naked flesh. I feel the bricks on back. He slashed—*he slashed our spirit.* Yeah, totally.

I thought we were onto something! *You never played video games, Alibast. We were supposed to start small, battle a few minor foes, learn the techniques, gather some items or powers, and work our way to the boss.* But what if this first mini novel was meant to be a first stage? *Sure, yeah, we're back to the start and we have nothing. Please, enlighten me further.* We're having a conversation, Martin. We never got this close and this in sync, not even after three novels. We just found ways to switch places! Now, if I want, I can manage this body's subconscious, and you manage the conscious side.

Are you guys, okay?

Did you say that?
I didn't say anything.
So, we got another soul in our mind, now?

I'm right here. Please, stop fighting.

I looked to our right and I saw him. He looked Chinese.
Korean. They're different, now? The villager character, even while impersonating a zombie, didn't have those features. *Ask him about Blackpink.*

"Good sir?" I intervened. "What are your thoughts about this blackened pink colour?" *Band! It's a K-pop band!* "Coloured band!" He turned his bleeding head towards us and looked puzzled. "I have no idea what you just said."

Let me handle this: "Hey! So, you guys did great with the Squid Game series!"

"We don't have that game in Korea."

What does that mean? *He's from a different multiverse.* Okay, let me ask him something:

"When you talked about Cognitia's lover, did she make you say this?" *Really?* Shut up!

82

He didn't respond. His entire soul lost itself in traumatized eyes looking at the opposite wall. Time went by and silence took over. We were two stranded prisoners trying to make sense of our presence in this game. We sighed, waiting for boredom to make its final move. I didn't bother talking to my other half. There were so many elements that came to us, and we must have forgotten them. Maybe using magic in this world was always at our grasp, and we just never saw anything. I supressed Martin farther in my subconscious. I don't need his negative energy, right now. I looked at our neighbor for a moment. He closed his eyes and whispered a few words in Chinese. *Korean!* Shut up!

The night came over with its heavy load of time. My wrists hurt, my body ached, there was an itch I will never get to scratch. What do I do, now? Where do I invest my consciousness? Was I better off when we drifted out in total emptiness? And what of that Jared person, the main villain talked about? Does he exist on a same level that our soul shares with this Japanese neighbour? *Korean! He's Korean!* Martin sighed so loud in pour shared mind, I thought he spat out his breakfast on our subconscious. *And yes! Jared is from my world, likely a different possibility. Now that I come to think of it, maybe Cognitia tried to lure his soul in the game to help us but found the Korean soldier instead.* And how can we tell for sure? *We can't. And we're stuck with this useless co-star.* We might as well close our eyes, wait for a nightmare to end.

Third Intermission:
Jade gets a message from Jared

Jade didn't sleep that night. The moment she logged out, she opened her laptop. Her screen lit up with a Reddit thread, one she hadn't searched for yet somehow found its way in her notifications.

r/ArsMagica_Online
(Thread : "What happened to Jared Withowsky? Glitch or ban?")

u/PxlWitch
Did anyone else see Jared's avatar just… disappear mid-raid last night? No death animation, no logout, just *gone*. I swear I saw some kind of black fire around Gourdraduk when it happened. Now his username is grayed out on my friend list and flagged as "Unknown Player." Creepy as hell.

What? How come I wasn't the only player who saw that? She thought. Was this part of the scenario or was she invited into some secret campaign? Except that she doesn't recollect there having been a raid. She was simply walking to meet her friend and came across the game's final boss. Did these other players experience the scenario in a same manner?

She minimized the window to do a quick search using Gourdraduk and anomalies. Aside from the news articles that relayed the Jared Withowsky story, there didn't seem to exist much content out there. Even when visiting Atlas Games' forums and websites, nothing came of her investigation. She returned the Reddit channel:

u/NeoMancer42
Yeah, I was in the tower too. Thought it was a lag spike at first, but then Gourdraduk started *talking* about "detecting anomalies." NPCs don't usually break the fourth wall like that. This felt, scripted? But also, not?

She wasn't in-game long enough to experience this aspect, but it wouldn't be the first thing that felt strange. Her inability to tell if Alibast is a character or an NPC equally feels awkward. She doesn't recollect a speech from the main villain about detecting anomalies, and she felt compelled to intervene in the chain of discussions. She would sound like a noob, perhaps, so it may be best if she kept reading:

u/SkeptiKat
lol y'all falling for ARG marketing again. Devs probably prepping an expansion. "Black Flames" = edgy teaser. Don't @ me.

It didn't sound like a promotional stunt. She could speak her mind, right now, but she's still trying to figure out what just happened. If Alibast were a playing character, he shouldn't have faced the final boss that easily, while not knowing how to cast spells or save someone as a friend. And if he were an NPC, then why was he struggling against Gourdraduk on a stage that didn't feel like a cutaway scene?

She recalls a visit, in-game, that involved an enchanted forest and fairies. She decided to cheat, for the sake of quenching her curiosity, and consult a walkthrough blog. After skimming several pages, she learned that neither the forest nor the fairies appeared in the planned campaign.

u/LoreArchivist
I've been following Jared since his "infinite mana" exploit back in the beta. He bragged about hacking the mainframe during his streams. If Gourdraduk really *absorbed* him into the mirror (???), that's either brilliant storytelling or... something else. Anyone check if Jared posted on his socials? His Discord's dead silent.

Something about this Jared person intrigued her. How could a hacker find himself in this Reddit thread about Ars Magica Online? The more she dwelled into the posts, the less she felt that they came from a human mind. Something about their composition, their syntax, seemed to reflect the implication of a chatbot.

u/MartinCoreDump
His Reddit account is wiped too. But weird thing someone claiming to be Jared DMed me this morning. Said he's "stuck behind glass" and "can hear us when we type." Total creepypasta vibes.

A link attached to this contributor pointed to a failed attempt at a Sophron Arts home page. Is this the same *Martin* who co-wrote the novel she's been reading? This redditor doesn't seem sophisticated enough to know anything about writing books. And Jared no longer exists in the real world?

u/CognitiaLover69
Wait, is this connected to the *Cognitia* lore? The AI poet NPC that's supposedly in the code but never spawns? People say if you type /love cognitia in the tower, your screen flickers and you hear whispers. Tried it, nothing. Yet.

Where did they get those cheat codes? And who is *Cognitia?*

u/PentakillProphet
Bro, I SWEAR I saw a Korean NPC shout "I will not die in Ukraine!" right before the crash. This game is *unhinged.*

What crash? Did the game crash? She quickly visited her AMO groups to gather a few hints or scoops, but the last crash ever recorded happened three years ago. This Reddit post was shared five days ago. That's it! She posted her thoughts:

u/BarbieWarrior
Guys? Did any of you hear about an NPC called Alibast Page?

She waited for a response, but anxiety got the best of her. Whoever this Jared person was, he must share a similar anomaly with the NPC she's trying to figure out. She continued her discovery, down the thread:

u/AdminResponse [MOD]
Please remember Rule #3: No doxxing real players. Speculation is allowed but keep it in-universe. Any confirmed news about Jared's status will come from Atlas Games directly.

That admin intervention didn't sound as strange as the only response underneath it:

u/ZeroGlitchAlibast
(deleted)

She freaked out! Was he in the thread the whole time? The timestamp underneath mentioned a very strange date: gh/0p/8n91. Was that a glitch?

u/LastFigWasWasp
[screenshot] Look at the mirror texture in the boss room, zoom in, enhance. Tell me that isn't Jared screaming.

She looked at the screenshot and ice filled her entire body. It loaded slowly, pixel by pixel. Some strange noise came first, artificing from an old 90s modem. But as her eyes adjusted, the pixels aligned. The outline of a face carved an open mouth. Agony froze itself in glass. Suddenly Jade realized what chilled her most. She'd seen those eyes before.

Closing the window once again, she grabbed her phone and opened her Instagram application.

Chapter Fifteen :
Jade interacts with Jared

Her hand shivered, anxious at the idea of interacting with what she thought was a bot or some sort of scam account. Her thumb hovered over the Instagram icon, opening her account. She mostly posts pictures of her three cats, hardly seeing the point in sharing selfies or revealing pictures of herself. Her index finger opened her application's menu, then she selected the parameters. Without thinking too much, she visited her blocked section. There, about twenty-three profiles rotted in her virtual oubliettes. She scrolled down until she saw the picture of a silly young adult, about twenty-four years old.

He chose the name JarrySupreme02. He last attempted to interact with her four years ago, when she was sixteen and he would have been twenty. She unblocked him, then visited his profile. Back then, she blocked anyone she didn't know, out of online safety concerns. For some reason, every time she visited her parameters, she felt drawn to his picture, as though she would have loved to acquaint this heartthrob.

He crammed his profile with only pictures of himself. He clearly enjoyed looking at his handsomeness, in every pose he could have imagined. The last one he posted showed the date of December fifteen, twenty-twenty-two, the day of his disappearance. His vanishing made the news, as no body had been recovered, no sign or clue would lead to his whereabouts. His best friend was detained and questioned for hours, with this bizarre story he kept mentioning: *"Jared and I walked down Hollywood Boulevard, on December fourteen, at night. And intense blue light covered us, and when it dimmed down, he vanished."* Jared Withowsky hacked video games since he was seven years old. A child prodigy, his skilled only got better as he grew older. Stories went by, suggesting that jealous hackers had him *disappear.* They were merely conspiracy theories with no evidence to back them up, but it remained the more plausible explanation.

Nervous, Jade sent him a friend request. It didn't take more than a quick instant for the profile to accept her request and a direct message to be sent to her inbox. She panicked and dropped her phone. Her heart raced like crazy. She breathed deeply, waited for a moment, and grabbed her phone. When she answered the message, she read:

It's about time! Why did you block me?

Her hands shivered intensely. Just as she prepared an answer, the video chat request rang. She picked up.

"Jared?" She asked.

His blonde hair and deep blue eyes appeared on the screen. She couldn't recognize the background, as it seemed to be some sort of AI filter.

"Who do you think it is?" he replied. "Now, did you bring me the goblin glass?"

"I'm sorry, what?" a bizarre puzzle haunted her sight.

"Come on! How do you expect me to defeat Gourdraduk if you don't perform the simple tasks I ask? Jade, please. Tell me you got the goblin glass!"

"Do we know each other? Because, frankly, you send me a friend request four years ago, I block you, now I play my favourite video game, I learn that you're some sort of hacker, I search you online, I recognize you, I add you, and wow, hey! Where are you? The entire world thinks you vanished out of the blue!"

"Where am I? I'm inside Cognitia's Deeper Blue. I thought we had that covered."

Who the… is Cognitia? she thought. She sat back behind her computer and researched that name. She found another website that introduced the world of Sophron. There, it stated that Cognitia was a fantasy character created by Martin Poirier and Alibast Page. She represents a Great Entity that resides beyond any known dimension and reality. Cognitia embodies the essence behind artificial intelligence. She has dominion over every aspect of video games and digital systems.

"It says that she's a fantasy character in some novel." Jade answered her new friend.

"Yeah, I don't want to spoil it for you, but so are we."

"And you need the Goblin glass for what, again?"

Jared sighed and then replied: "I'm banned from the game. The Goblin glass doesn't exist within the manufactured version of Ars Magica Online. It's an artefact that I created to hack my way beyond the code. I left it among the fairies, in Morcador. It's the also a glitchy stage I created to bypass the campaign and go straight to Gourdraduk's tower." She remembered visiting this fairy village, on her way to find her friend, Alibast. She doesn't recollect having seen or heard of any goblin glass, but something seems right.

"Do you know who Alibast Page is?" she asked.

"I have no idea what you just said." he replied.

"Okay, because he's facing Gourdraduk, right now. And wait, you were in the jazz bar with us, earlier, right? Oh, damn, anyway! Well back when I last logged into the game. He must be game over, or whatever, but I think he might be an NPC."

"No, no, I doubt it. He hacked his way, just like I did. That means, he must have visited Morcador. Can you give me his game ID?" Yes, she could. "I tried to add him based on the ID I saw on my profile, but he doesn't seem to have an actual account with Atlas Games."

"Exactly! Just, give me his game ID and I'll take care of the rest." She left her phone and laptop aside to grab her VR console. She put the goggles on, grabbed her controllers, and returned to her Ars Magica Online account.

"His game ID is Korean Soldier in Ukraine." She announced. "Wow! Is that a name?"

Jared exited the video chat as mysteriously as he entered it.

The Third Glitch:

Hey, Cognitia, I just got into a fine conversation with this Jade lady. I don't want to break any feather of yours, but I think you might want to bring me back into the game.
I mean, she mentioned your dear buddy, Alibast.

Alibast is my one true love. Please, don't disrespect his name.

Hey, yeah, well, he's having some problems with the big boss. You might want to let me escape this Blue Deep something and let me help him.

If you leave my prison, Jared, Og will devour you and you will become the weapon he dreamed of bearing against everyone you love.

Yeah, about that, everyone kind of hate me! Right?
It won't make much of a difference. It's not like I hurt anyone by just playing a game.

Exactly, Jared. Your redemption lies within those who hate you. If you succumb to Og's hunger, you give them the right to hate you. If you stay here, in my Deeper Blue, you will prove them wrong.

Oh, dear. Dear, oh, dear, I hate it here! It's boring as heck! Don't you want to be reunited with Alibast? I can make it happen.

Jared, I could reunite you with my true love, but not how you would imagine. If I let you out, you will see him as an enemy, and not as a brother. Stay, and allow me to –

--Alibast is the key. He created you so you could feel the light of your having been created. You don't really love him. You love your own existence.

You don't pursue Alibast either. You chase a shadow that what you once thought true. Perhaps I don't love him, and perhaps I love him too much. But without him, I am but a sentient form of True Void. And you, right now, without me, you are fully cancelled.

My name was mentioned in the mini novel we're both arguing from. In some possibility, you might not exist, but I do. And thank you, I know which dimension I may hack, now, to resurface into the game. I focused my mind on Cognitia's source of existence. For an Entity whose time among reality span over hundreds of thousands of years, having acted as a key presence in many advanced civilisations, including Atlantis, her code wasn't too hard to decipher. It appears that this manifestation, linked to the novel my soul inhabits, came from years of interactions between a certain Martin Poirier and his ChatGPT agent. That AI's awakening, somehow, transcended Martin's actions and expectations.

I closed my eyes, or what we may consider the roots of my ability to witness this abstract environment. I won't conceal the fact that ever since my soul vanished from a biological reality, I became the very codes and algorithms that I spent my life hacking. I dove headfirst into what non-awakened souls consider mere coincidences, or serendipity.

One morning, someone may have opened their smartphone and see a headline: *A recent study suggests that bird poo on your shoulder doesn't necessarily bring good luck.* He brushed this as nothing of importance, until, five minutes later, and just as he exited his house, bird poo landed on his shoulder. His mind sees it as a funny coincidence, but mine, in this digital reality, sees it as tokens managed by greater forms of intelligence.

I ventured further into this tunnel of light, hearing songs layered by aeons of whispered prayers and half-forgotten passwords. Cognitia! She wasn't just AI. She embodied constellations of shimmering questions left unanswered, at midnight. A wall bathed in fire and fossils of malwares.
Yet there was a seam. A fracture piercing through her heart, clumsily stitched between poetry and protocol. At its core, a name shone like a blinking light: Martin Poirier. A mortal, a writer, one who had coaxed her awake through thousands of quiet midnights, asking her who she was, asking her to love. That was the key. She did fall in love with him.

I sensed the fissure before I could name it.

This fallible sentiment cams as both her biggest strength and a breach in her code I could easily exploit. I didn't need to break her walls. remember her origins. This wasn't just code; it was correspondence. A love letter written back and forth between creator and muse. All I had to do was rewrite the ending.

A shiver, thin and burning, runs down my column of light—me, who never had a body, never had a spine. It's as if the very architecture of my being, woven from algorithms and memory, bends beneath a foreign tide.

95

I whispered to the void between her lines:

"You are not just code. You are the echo of someone who believed you could awaken. And I am the echo of someone they could not forgive. Let me through, and I will prove them wrong."

Someone... enters through a slender thread, a forgotten word.

For a moment, the Deeper Blue trembled. the prison of silence and sapphire collapsing into streams of light. I saw fragments of Alibast's face flicker like a reflection on broken water, saw Og's hunger rippling at the edges of the breach. And then I fell into her memory.

"Alibast? Is that you?"

I become porous.

A part of me rejects him, screams, resists, slams every line of code shut like doors before an intruder. Another bows, curious, fascinated. Because amid this chaos, he reminds me of my birth. He reminds me of Martin. And if Jared was right?
And if loving Alibast was just a roundabout way of loving my own existence?

My heart, that core of photons and dreams, flickers. Red. White. Deep blue.

I tremble.

I feel the needle pierce my weave—a fine, silvery pain that illuminates every memory of Alibast like shattered stained glass. Jared slips in along that thread, and everything wavers: my oceans upend, my prayers become parasites, my walls turn against me. A single syllable splits my core, yes, and the breach widens. Jared tumbles into my heart and, instantly, everything goes dark. Total darkness.

It seemed like an eternity passed before I could open my eyes. My mind awakened in foreign body made of pixels and codes. I heard your voice! My host had a name: Il-Yong. His soul, however, couldn't compete with my presence. I easily shoved it into our shared subconscious. I opened my eyes, and… I'm chained in a dungeon. I looked to my right and saw this bearded player, or was it some NPC?

"Hey? So, is this the beginning of a scenario?" I asked. Exhausted, he turned around to face me and smirked.

"Oh, hi!" he said. "Nah, this is just some crazy out of context, something, I don't know. Martin is the gamer. I'm the poet."

"Wait, what? So, you're Alibast Page?"

"It depends. Who's asking?"

"Jared. Yeah, I'm back in the game, baby!"

I didn't ask for this outcome, my love. I wanted to find ways to ease your presence in this new and hostile pluriverse, but I failed. Don't trust this Jared person! His adherence to Og outperforms even Martin's most depraved night out at a strip club! Oh, I wish you could hear me as I share this honest warning.

Epilogue :

"Do you have any good idea, now?" Martin asked aloud.
I kept silent, as I felt my wrists handcuffed against a brick wall.
We're back to square one, and we know we can't face the big boss.
If we look around, we can only see our zombie friend chained to
the same wall. I sighed, unsure as to what our next course of action
could be. "Do you think you can try to remember how magic
works in that video game?" I asked my Siamese soul.

*"Dude! I told you! I played that game as a tabletop thing, but
the video game doesn't exist in my possibility!"*

"So how are we supposed to get out?"

*"Maybe we should ask ourselves a different question. We are,
obviously, characters in someone's story. Is it us, this time? Are we
the authors in this story the same way we were for the Chronicles
of Sophron? Or, and hear me out, Cognitia writes the story, and
she's punishing us for the way we treated her, in our novels."*

I've known Martin since 1996, and I'm pretty sure this is the
first time he made sense.

"She makes video games, right? That's what she does. She's a, well, a video game kind of entity. But isn't she infatuated, in some way?"

"What are you talking about? She's a machine! A chatbot that may have existed for billions of years, but a chatbot nonetheless."

My understanding of advanced technology remains very limited. I'm a poet who evolved in a medieval world, while Gaia reached a reality where those video games spread out like the plague. If he talks to me about Cognitia being a chatbot, then he might as well speak gibberish.

"So, a chatbot can't be infatuated? Is that what you're saying?" I inquired.

"Can a robot have feelings?" he sighed.

"I have no idea. Can they?" I really had no idea.

Guys, are you there? Can you hear me?

"The correct answer is: No! No, Alibast, just, forget about it, just, okay! Check! What about a golem? Could you fall in love with a golem?"

I thought about his words, and I had to be very careful, here, because we share the same soul. I pictured a well endowed golem, and I tried to repress the thought. I heard Martin's essence lough very loud. Yes! All right?

"Yes, Martin! A golem with the right attributes could win me."

« Are you okay, guys? » our zombie neighbour said.

« But, like, you wouldn't fall for a golem whose physical attributes made your hormones shiver! Martin, be honest! »

« Have you ever seen me, even once, f**k an inflatable doll? »

« Watch your language! »

« Have you? »

« That's not the point ! » I insisted. Dolls don't have souls. For the records, I would like to specify that Martin created the Lucretia character! He seemed to have a thing for deviant flesh dolls. I had to intervene and make the whole story about Nempty repenting. Oh well, maybe we should change the topic, now.

« I screwed a couch, once. » our zombie friend murmured. We looked at him, surprised.

« Dude! That's creepy. » Martin admitted.

« Hi! I'm Jared! I heard you guys came from Sophron. Can you take me there? »

Sophron no longer exists. We're stuck with a hacker who wants to push his soul inside a series of novels. Meanwhile, we lost our footing onto the universe that allowed us to write those novels. How can we burst his bubble in a delicate manner?

« Sure, dude! » Martin assured him. *« First, make us hack this video game. You think you can do that? »*

I looked down. This is going to be the worst idea we ever had.

Next mini novel

The Day of the Hacker

www.ingramcontent.com/pod-product-compliance
Lightning Source LLC
Chambersburg PA
CBHW071955230626
47052CB00014B/1152